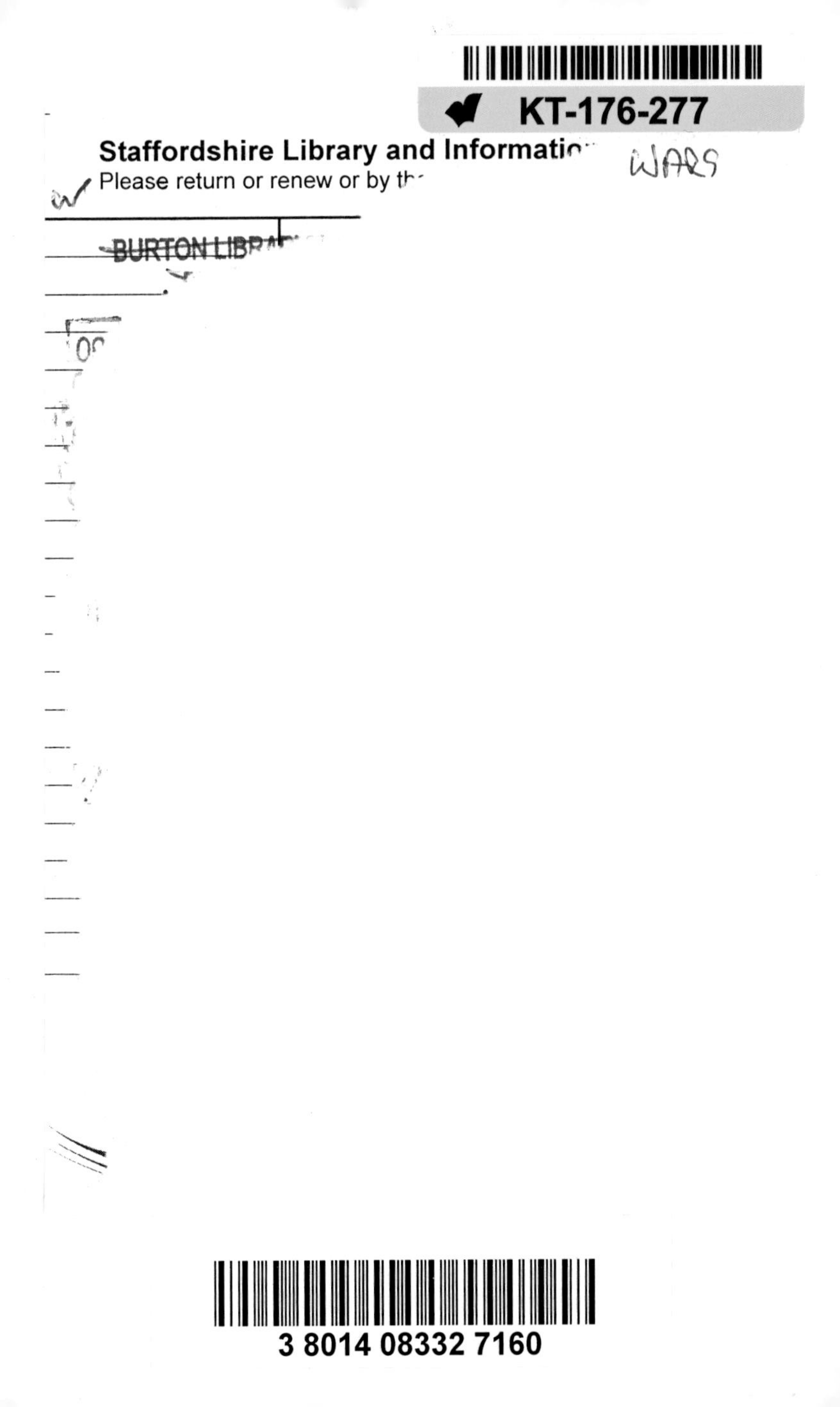

Outlaw Queen

An outlaw gang known as the Starrbreakers has been causing mayhem in the territory of Wyoming. After each robbery, the bandits quickly vanish into the stronghold of the Big Horn Mountains through a mysterious gap known as Hole in the Wall.

The usual law authorities have been rendered powerless to hunt the Starrbreakers down so Special Agent Drew Henry has been hired to infiltrate the gang in the guise of an escaped convict.

Bullets are set to fly when Drew Henry comes to town. Can he take on the Outlaw Queen and curtail the Starrbreakers' stranglehold?

By the same author

Dead Man Walking
Two for Texas
Divided Loyalties
Return of the Gunfighter
Dynamite Daze
Apache Rifles
Duel at Del Norte

Writing as Dale Graham

High Plains Vendetta
Dance with the Devil
Nugget!
Montezuma's Legacy
Death Rides Alone
Gambler's Dawn
Vengeance at Bittersweet
Justice for Crockett
Bluecoat Renegade

Outlaw Queen

Ethan Flagg

ROBERT HALE · LONDON

First published in Great Britain 2011

ISBN 978-0-7090-9147-9

Robert Hale Limited
Clerkenwell House
Clerkenwell Green
London EC1R 0HT

www.halebooks.com

Typeset by
Derek Doyle & Associates, Shaw Heath
Printed and bound in Great Britain by
CPI Antony Rowe, Chippenham and Eastbourne

ONE

PAYROLL SNATCH

It was 9.45 on a fine Wednesday morning in the year 1877.

The fawning bank manager's head bobbed like a nodding donkey as he kowtowed to the graceful personage before him. 'My colleagues and I very much appreciate that you have decided to deposit all receipts from the Bee Hive with our bank, Miss Sherman.'

Belle accepted the unctuous civility with a slight tilt of the head. She presented the starchy image of a successful businesswoman, but with a gentle touch of vulnerability that all men favour. Bedecked in a shimmering gown of emerald-green silk that accentuated her large eyes, she had the little fat man just where she wanted him. In the palm of her hand, ensnared like a rabbit under the hypnotic allure of a rattlesnake.

As if in a dream, Harvey Tattler accepted the glass of Scotch whisky, avidly toasting their newly created association. Belle had invited the banker up to her private quarters ostensibly to discuss security of funds held by the Wyoming Central Reserve.

This was his second visit. Tattler had previously described the financial institution as being well nigh impossible to rob. After hearing about the security options in force, Belle had been compelled to abandon any ideas of a frontal assault.

But there was one point where funds were vulnerable. This was what she wanted to expand upon now.

'Let us hope that it will be the start of a fruitful and rewarding partnership,' the manager purred with a hint of expectancy that something other than business might be in the offing. Belle easily read the banker's carnal aspirations.

She ignored the thinly veiled pass. If the odious toad chose to entertain that notion, then he was spitting into the wind. But she kept such lugubrious thoughts to herself. The sugar-coated smile remained pasted across her captivating features.

'I take it that the transfer of funds to your head office will be suitably well guarded?' The enquiry was uttered in a lofty, somewhat imperious tone. 'There are a lot of bandits around these days. I would hate for my hard-earned dollars to be lost in transit.'

Tattler rubbed his hands, his small mouth hanging open. Bulging eyes that were absorbing the immodest display of cleavage suddenly became aghast that such a disaster could ever occur under his management.

'Have no fear, Miss Sherman,' he enthused. 'After the money has been loaded on to a wagon at the bank's rear exit, it will then be driven round to the front. Four guards will be waiting there to conduct it all the way to Cheyenne.' He slurped the whisky with noisy appreciation. 'Nobody would be foolish enough to attempt a robbery under such a heavily armed escort.'

'And the wagon departs promptly every Wednesday at noon?'

'On the dot!' pronounced the confident banker.

'Then I think our business is concluded, Mr Tattler,' replied Belle, emitting a sigh of confident assurance as she ushered the man out of her office above the Bee Hive saloon. A plan was already forming in her head. 'The first deposit will be made next week, if that is ageeable?'

'Certainly,' the banker concurred. 'And now perhaps you might consider another drink to seal our business?' Tattler's oily suggestion was accompanied by a hopeful leer. 'So we can get to know each other . . . erm' – a brief pause followed – 'on more intimate terms?'

'Nothing I would like better,' purred Belle, enveloping the little man with an overindulgent smile. Hope momentarily illuminated the simpering banker's beaming face, only to be snuffed out as she added, 'Unfortunately, I have promised Merv Rankin of the Flying V that I would look at some cattle he wants to sell. Business before pleasure. I'm sure you understand.'

'Another time then,' responded the deflated banker as the door closed on his rotund form.

'Perhaps,' came back the muffled, though less than enthusiastic answer.

'It's all fixed then?'

The gruff demand came from a big raw-boned hardcase.

Deftly rolling a quirley with one hand, Leroy Starr flipped the thin white tube skyward, caught it between his teeth and lit up with a vesta scratched against his faded blue Levis. A series of perfect smoke rings completed the showy manoeuvre.

Leroy bossed an outlaw band that he had nick-named the Starrbreakers.

It was an hour later. The hard-faced road agent was leaning against the wall of Belle's office, which faced on to the main street of Kaycee. His black eyes gleamed with appreciation, lustfully appraising the elegant contours of his companion.

Belle Sherman gave her thick red hair an arrogant toss. She was now dressed in range gear. A change of apparel had quickly followed the departure of the bank manager, but not for the purpose of visiting the Flying V.

'Bet yuh had that tub of lard eatin' outa your hand,' continued Starr, puffing out another smoke ring. In a more forceful tone he pressed, 'So did the skunk confirm arrangements for the shipment?'

Belle shrugged her slim shoulders.

'What do you think?'

There was no need for an answer.

Sauntering across to a full-length mirror, she carefully pinned up her thick mane beneath a wide-brimmed grey Stetson. Studying her reflection with a critical gaze, she tilted the hat to one side, giving a nod of satisfaction. Only the most eagle-eyed bystander would recognize her as the coquettish owner of the largest saloon in Kaycee.

Over the years the town had prospered due to a close association with the KC ranch. The name had stuck when other businesses had moved into the area. Belle had arrived in the Wyoming cattle town six months previously with the intention of investing in a lucrative venture.

The Bee Hive was up for grabs. But it wasn't the *For Sale* notice that had attracted her attention. A loose smile played across the svelte contours of her face as she perused an adjacent sign nailed to the outside wall. Encased in a colourful frame of sweet-smelling honeysuckle, it read:

Within the hive we're all alive
  Good whiskey makes us funny,
So if you're dry come in and try
  The flavour of our honey.

The strikingly attractive woman couldn't resist the offer.

So without further ado, she sauntered casually through the open door. The arrival of such an eye-catching visitor stunned the patrons into an awestruck silence. Belle had that effect on men. And she used it to her advantage.

The deal was concluded within the hour. Belle Sherman became the proud owner of a prosperous saloon. She now had a base from which to branch out into more clandestine and infinitely more lucrative enterprises: moneymaking schemes that would have the more sober citizens of Kaycee gasping in amazement had they known, or even suspected her intentions.

Once the Bee Hive was operating to her satisfaction, Belle had sent word for Leroy Starr and his bunch to join her. The gang had become too well-known to the law in their home stamping ground of Missouri. Heading west into the wild, untamed badlands of the Rockies was the perfect answer.

Happening across the hidden valley known as Hole in the Wall had been the icing on the cake.

'Even in that get-up, you still look a million dollars,' enthused the outlaw, lewdly surveying the finished product. 'All the same, I'd much prefer to see you without—'

'Cut the blarney, Leroy!' interjected the girl sharply. 'We ain't got time for that kinda talk.'

She was well aware of the direction in which her rough-and-ready associate's earthy leanings hoped to develop.

So far, the outlaw queen had managed to brush aside Starr's coarse attempts at romance with blithe disregard. After all, she was the boss of this outfit, the one with the brains. As such, she had no intention of getting involved with the hired help. At least, not until she was good and ready.

And this certainly wasn't the time. Nor would it ever be where Leroy Starr was concerned. But it did no harm to keep the poor sap dangling like a landed trout. A flirtatious smile from beneath lowered eye-brows always served to calm the gang boss's libido.

Belle cast a poignant eye towards the clock merrily ticking away on the wall. It read eleven o'clock.

'We've got an hour before the payroll leaves the bank,' she hurried on, drawing the pearl-handled Colt Frontier and expertly thumbing the cylinder to check the loading. 'Go down to the bar and gather the boys together. Make sure they know exactly what's expected. I'll meet you out back with the horses.' The serious frown returned as she added, 'And keep the rotgut on ice. I want everyone sharp as tacks for this caper.'

Starr just stood there. Affecting a casual disdain, he stubbed out the quirley and lit up a fine Havana cigar. A plume of blue smoke filtered from between yellow-stained teeth.

Belle's green eyes soured. Her lips were drawn tight over a perfect set of snow-white teeth. The lithe frame, slim and whipcord lean, brooked no dissent.

'Well?' she rapped out curtly. 'What in thunder are you waiting for? Christmas?'

The blunt command was issued by a woman used to being obeyed. And any man Jack who challenged her authority did so at his peril. Some had tried, to their eternal cost.

Brad Mason had balked at taking orders from a woman. He had declared as much in front of the entire gang the previous month at their Hole in the Wall hideout. It was a blatant challenge that Belle could not ignore. Her tough reputation was at stake.

She defied the guy to put his gun where his mouth was. Brad had laughed, figuring a woman had no chance against a hard-bitten tough like him.

'Bossing a gang ain't no job for a woman,' sneered Mason. 'Stick to what you're good at in the kitchen and the bedroom. That's what I say.'

The atmosphere in the log cabin crackled with suppressed tension. The others waited, expectantly, eager to see how this played out.

The girl maintained an aloof coolness, her eyes steely and oozing menace as she squared off before the lumbering ox. In a voice barely above a sibilant hiss, she said, 'Well then, slap leather, you son of a sidewinder. Or so help me I'll gun you down where you stand.'

Belle's blunt defiance removed the leering grin from Mason's face.

'If'n that's what you want, missy.'

His beefy shoulders lifted in a nonchalant shrug. Then he went for his gun. It never saw the light of day. Two shots rang out. Each chunk of lead found its mark in the braggart's chest. Mason was dead before his punctured body hit the floor.

'Any more of you guys figure to push this little gal aside?' The assured tone of Belle's blunt invitation was received in stunned silence. Brittle eyes, cold and hard as diamonds, along with the threatening revolver, panned the assembled band of outlaws.

And even a jasper of Leroy Starr's reputation knew when to hold his peace.

'OK, OK! I'm going,' muttered Starr, levering himself off the wall. He fastened a serious eye on to the vision of beauty. Both of them knew that each needed the other. Brawn versus brains. 'One of these days, you'll come to the understanding that I'm the only guy for you, Belle. Sooner you cotton to that notion the better.'

Starr didn't wait for a reply. Stamping out of the opulent inner sanctum of the bandit queen, he headed downstairs into the bar.

'I wouldn't hold your breath, Leroy.' The curt utterance was accompanied by a barked grunt of derision. 'You'll be waiting a long time.'

Five minutes before the church clock was due to chime the noon hour, six hard-nosed gunmen were waiting behind the bank.'

'Check your weapons, boys.' The terse command was issued by Leroy Starr. 'And make sure those masks are tight.'

Belle always deferred to her second-in-command when the gang were engaged on a job. The boys preferred it, even though they knew where the real power lay. Adjusting her own bandanna, the woman blended perfectly with the other robbers. Only the most acute observer would have recognized the smouldering green eyes of the Bee Hive's glamorous owner behind the face mask.

A snarling mutt broke through the tension and began snapping at the heels of one of the mounts.

Rusty Laverne growled out an ungodly curse while grabbing for the pistol on his hip. Another hand shot out and enveloped his clutching paw in a grip of steel.

'Don't think on it, knucklehead.' rasped Starr, fastening a bleak eye on the young tough. 'D'yuh wanna bring the whole durned town on our necks?'

'S-sorry about that, boss,' stuttered the contrite gunslinger. 'Weren't thinkin' straight.' Laverne had only recently joined forces with the Starrbreakers. Although he had already killed five men, this was his first outing with the new gang. He was feeling a touch nervous.

Starr merely grunted in reply as he launched a thin stiletto that skewered the recalcitrant mutt in its tracks. He was just in time.

The rear door of the bank had just opened. A troop of suited officials filed out escorting the heavy iron-bound strongbox, which was lifted into the bed of a wagon. The hovering bank manager stood to one side as he pompously supervised the loading. Satisfied that the box was hidden beneath a tarpaulin cover, Harvey Tattler then returned to his office.

Jeb Stokes, the driver, lit up a smoke before leathering the team of four into motion. Once the back lot was vacated the old driver turned to the right. A narrow alleyway twisted in dogleg fashion before merging with the main street of town. Hidden from view, here was the bank's Achilles' heel.

That was when the gang pounced.

'Haul up there, fella,' rasped a harsh growl muffled behind the mask. At the same time the wagon was surrounded by the other bandits. 'One false move and you're dead meat.'

Stokes was no hero, and this wasn't his dough.

'Don't shoot, mister,' he pleaded as both hands shot skywards. 'I ain't about to give you guys any trouble.' He didn't even glance towards the Loomis shotgun perched beside his trembling torso. With only two years to go before he drew his pension, Stokes had every intention of doing just that.

Starr was not convinced. He gave the driver no chance to regain his nerve. A single blow to the head with the butt end of his revolver and Stokes was laid out cold. He slumped backwards into the bed of the wagon.

As previously arranged, Vic Stride and Bitter Creek Watson jumped into the the wagon. Roughly toeing aside the driver's unconscious body, they lifted the heavy box and secured it across the saddle of a spare mount.

All six then swung their horses round and galloped off down the alley in the direction away from the main street. Twisting and turning amidst the chaotic array of shacks and detritus that littered this poorest quarter of Kaycee, the gang disappeared in a flurry of dust. The hard pace was maintained until they were well beyond the town limits.

Belle's precision planning had allowed five

minutes before the robbery was discovered and the alarm raised. Another fifteen for the sheriff to swear in a posse. Plenty of time for the Starrbreakers to vanish into the maze of draws and gulches that filtered rainfall down to swell the waters of the Powder River.

Past the soaring pinnacle of Deadman's Butte, they headed through the Roughneck Range. Here they were forced down to single file and walking pace while negotiating the narrow gap that gave access to Hole in the Wall.

It was late afternoon when they eventually made it through. There before them, stretching away into the distance, lay the hidden hollow known as Buffalo Creek.

'Yeehaaaah!'

Once through the narrow gateway to the secret valley, Laverne could contain his excitement no longer. The raucous halloo was accompanied by a gleeful waving of his hat in the air. Spurring his mount to a furious gallop, the young tearaway cut a neat swath through the ocean of waving grass cloaking the valley floor.

The others quickly joined in the boisterous celebration as they caught up. Pounding in line abreast, they raced each other towards the log cabin. It was erected on a terrace beneath the red cliffs lining the far side of the valley.

Once the horses had been fed and watered a liquid celebration, involving the best Scotch whisky supplied by Belle, was enjoyed by everybody.

All, that is, except for the outlaw queen, who left early to establish her alibi with the Flying V. That way, no possible suspicion regarding the robbery could fall upon the Bee Hive's sassy proprietor. After all, hadn't the bank manager been made fully aware that she would be out of town on cattle business when it had been perpetrated?

TWO

STICK-IN-THE-MUD

Two weeks had passed since the payroll robbery at Kaycee. The local tinstar had drawn a blank in his efforts to track down the culprits. Lurid headlines in the *Kaycee Epitaph*, pouring scorn on the inept handling of the affair, had not helped matters. In consequence and much to his chagrin, Heck Ramsey was forced to seek help from a higher authority.

An urgent meeting was convened at Laramie.

Leading officials in charge of law enforcement had been summoned to thrash out a strategy for tackling the lawlessness threatening to swamp the territory. This current spate of hold-ups was clearly not the work of ordinary bandits and desperadoes. The assembled notaries were most concerned that the culprits had seemingly just disappeared, apparently into thin air.

'These critters are too well organized,' emphasized a bluff, silver-headed jasper, puffing hard on a large cigar.

The stark exclamation came following a desultory conversation in which nothing positive regarding the problem had emerged. Thick grey eyebrows met in the middle of his forehead as he considered the dire situation. Judge Abel Ferman occupied a seat at the head of the long table in the main committee room above the town council offices. It was he who carried overall responsibility for the law in Wyoming.

'And they've gotta be stopped!' A clenched fist slammed down on the mahogany surface. Coffee cups rattled on their saucers, some of the contents spilling on to the polished surface of the table.

'Ain't no way that we can obtain full statehood with gangs of cutthroats roaming the territory unimpeded,' agreed Blake Chainey, the recently elected mayor of Laramie.

'Who's the local tinstar?' enquired the town's sheriff.

'A guy by the name of Heck Ramsey,' replied the judge, stroking his jutting chin. 'I chose him myself. If old Heck is stumped, then we sure got ourselves big trouble.'

'Yeah! A good man.' The sheriff gave a curt nod of agreement. 'I recall he was the fella that cleaned up Thermopolis two years back.'

'So what we gonna do about it?' queried the mayor, casting a bleak eye over the small gathering.

Blank faces stared back at him. Then a low, gravelly voice at the far end of the table broke the awkward silence.

'I might have the answer to your problem, gentlemen.'

The sudden announcement caused the other members of the council to turn their attention quizzically on to the speaker.

Isaac Thruxton had been thoughtfully listening to the heated discourse. He was head of a newly formed federal body whose remit was to coordinate law enforcement on a nationwide basis. The organization was called the Bureau of Advanced Detection. It was no surprise that agents assigned to serve the Bureau were quickly labelled the Bad Boys. It was an apt nickname.

A small man, rather insignificant to the casual observer, he nevertheless possessed an iron determination to root out skulduggery and transgressing at all levels. Thruxton had been given unlimited power to achieve this end and was answerable directly to the President himself. And Isaac intended to make full use of that authority.

His piercing blue gaze swept the room. Icy cold, his eyes immediately grabbed the attention of all whom they appraised. The wild hair and rather ill-kempt appearance went unheeded.

Slowly and with a deliberation intended to arouse puzzlement, Thruxton rose to his feet. Without a word, he strolled across to the office door, grasped the handle and gave the assemblage another somewhat enigmatic smirk. Then he opened the door.

'Allow me to present Mr Drew Henry.'

Standing to one side, he beckoned the visitor to

enter the room.

A large, raw-boned man stepped forward. The imposing figure blocked the doorway. In stark contrast to the meeting of dignitaries, this man was clad in dust-stained range garb. His age could have been anything between thirty and fifty. It was difficult to judge, as the square-jawed face was hidden behind dark stubble that had not witnessed a razor in two weeks.

But what attracted the gathering's attention was not the twin-holstered gun rig slung around the man's slim waist, but the hard, uncompromising gaze now staring them down. Drew Henry was clearly not a man who scared easily. He evoked the image of a one-man army.

No words were uttered by the mysterious stranger. It was left to Isaac Thruxton to make the introductions.

'Drew has ridden all the way from Denver at my personal request,' said the government agent. 'He is one of only a handful of operatives who have been specially chosen to undertake difficult assignments that are above and beyond the normal expectations of the regular lawmen.' Again his keen gaze panned the room. 'And I am sure we all agree that this situation is just such an occasion when his unique skills are in demand.'

It was Judge Ferman who broke the spell cast by the awesome presence standing before them.

'Perhaps you would care to enlighten us as to how this man is going, single-handedly, to defeat a gang of desperadoes that has thwarted every law enforcement agency in the territory.' The statement contained a hint of the sarcastic without, seemingly, giving offence.

Thruxton smiled. A knowing look passed between the two federal agents.

Henry flipped out a cigar from his buckskin jacket and lit up.

'You're better at words than me, Isaac,' drawled the stranger through a plume of blue smoke. 'Enlighten the gentlemen.'

Thruxton rested his hands on the table before glancing at each man in turn.

'Our plan is for Drew to assume the identity of a known outlaw. The man is serving time in the Colorado penitentiary,' he began, forcefully stressing each point with a jabbing finger. 'Beavertail Bob Luman is doing a ten-year stretch for armed robbery.'

'I've heard of that varmint,' interjected Sheriff Budd Shaeffer, narrowing his eyes in thought. 'A real evil character. Ain't he the skunk that shot Mel Travis in the back?'

'That's the one,' concurred Thruxton grimly. 'Travis was lucky to survive. That's why the skunk only got ten years. One of our men caught up with him at Steamboat Springs.'

'So what's the plan?' pressed Judge Ferman, steering the conversation back to the matter in hand. 'I assume that Luman ain't known in these parts, otherwise Henry here will get eyeballed before he's gotten any chance of getting near the gang.'

'We expect they'll have heard of his reputation,' replied Thruxton. 'Indeed, that's what we're counting on. But Luman hasn't ventured this far north before. So far he's kept to his own patch, only robbing stagecoaches and banks in Colorado and the northern reaches of New Mexico.'

'How you figuring to infiltrate the gang, Mr Henry?' enquired Budd Shaeffer, standing up and addressing the lounging gunfighter directly.

Henry levered himself off the wall and nipped the end of his cigar before replying. The Texan drawl was slow and measured, but delivered in a confidently quiet tone.

'My aim is to try to get close to the gang's secret hideout, then offer my services.' The agent paused, flicking a loose flake of tobacco from his lip. 'One man has a much better chance than an army of lawmen.' He then cast an eye towards his boss for confirmation. Thruxton took the hint.

'We reckon these boys will jump at the chance to have a dude with Beavertail Luman's reputation join their ranks,' he continued. 'Then once he's established, Drew here can start feeding us information about the gang's future plans. That way we can be ready to nail them good.'

He raised an eyebrow towards the gathered officers, seeking their support for the scheme.

'Well, I for one reckon this is our only hope,' averred the judge. 'Everyone else agree?'

Firm nods passed round the table as each member

of the committee gave his seal of approval.

'Then we're all agreed,' concluded Mayor Chainey, rising to his feet. 'Drew Henry is given our unqualified support in the apprehension of this vile gang of desperadoes.'

'We agree!' came back the unanimous reply.

'Be under no illusions, gentleman,' warned the solid gunfighter, purposefully drawing both his revolvers and twirling them expertly before slipping them back into their holsters. 'There's gonna be blood spilled, and some of it may belong to innocent victims.' A shrug followed the sombre warning. 'You can't make a good breakfast without breaking eggs.'

'Just try to keep them there guns of your'n pointed at the villains,' advised the judge with a grunt that was meant to lighten the bleak moment.

'I'll do my best,' said Henry.

'Then let's drink on it.' The mayor poured out shots of finest Scotch. They then toasted their new paladin.

'To a successful mission and the end of the Starrbreakers,' intoned Judge Ferman.

The next day found Drew Henry in the guise of Beavertail Bob Luman departing from Laramie with his broad back to the freshly laundered morning sun. As he headed north-west, his destination was the site of the most recent incursion by the Starr Gang. Kaycee was a five-day ride away, four if he pushed the big grey to its limits.

After crossing the Shirley Mountains on the final

day, he was jogging the horse through an ocean of grass that brushed against the grey's underquarters. Rolling countryside ideal for the raising of beef cattle stretched away to the distant horizon. Hidden from view behind a screen of dwarf willow, he suddenly came upon the wide depression occupied by the North Platte River.

But what caught his attention, even before the horse had nudged a passage through the dense thicket of trees, was a frightened scream. This was no plaintive warble. At first Drew figured it as the death throes of a hunted prairie dog. A second piercing yell curdled his blood.

It most definitely was of human origin, and of the female variety.

As he dug his spurs deep the grey bounded forward. Surging through the clinging branches and out on the far side, Drew immediately perceived the source of the terrifying clamour. A young woman was trapped up to her armpits in a cloying mud hole. Her panicked efforts to escape the lethal clutches of the morass were only making her situation more life-threatening.

Another minute and she would be totally smothered by the fetid ooze. There was only one course of action left. Drew leapt from the saddle and unhooked his lariat. Shaking the open end loose, he twirled it above his head.

'Raise your arms, miss,' he shouted to the struggling girl. 'And stop thrashing about like a hooked trout. You'll only sink deeper. When the loop drops over your head, grab it tightly and hang on.'

The panic-stricken female was almost beyond reason. Drew had forcefully to urge her to do as he ordered, stressing that this was her only hope of survival. The mud was already lapping at her chin.

Like a striking rattler, the plaited hide rope snaked out towards the stricken figure. Drew was well aware that this was the only chance he would get to save the girl from a grisly end.

He needn't have worried. His aim was perfection itself. The girl immediately gripped the rope as her saviour wrapped his own end around the grey's saddle horn. Then he slapped the horse on its rump, sending it scurrying up the bank.

At first it met solid opposition as the mud hole resisted any attempt to surrender its victim. But Snapper was a determined piece of horseflesh and tugged ever harder.

'Come on, old gal,' urged Drew. 'You can do it.'

The mare's efforts were rewarded by a sickening glug as the grasping quagmire was forced to yield up its prey. The girl slid across the soft marshy surface until a high-pitched whistle brought the charging animal to a sudden halt on the dry, sandy riverbank.

Drew hurried across. Carefully, he helped the panting girl to her feet.

'You OK?' he asked wiping the thick dollops of mud from her face. The sight revealed was most assuredly worth his clumsy ministrations. The girl was no plain-Jane. Even beneath the dripping rivulets of ooze that still gave her the appearance of an over-baked brownie cake, it was obvious she was as pretty as a Sunday picnic.

Unable to speak, she sucked in lungfuls of pure clean air while spitting out lumps of gritty sludge. It was another five minutes and copious gulps from Drew's water bottle before some sense of normality was restored.

'Gee, mister,' she gasped out at last, slumping down on the solid ground. 'If'n you hadn't come along when you did, I'd have surely been a goner.'

'Glad to have been of assistance,' murmured the good Samaritan. 'I was just passing on my way to find work in Kaycee.'

'Well, I'm sure glad you came to the Bighorn country,' smiled the girl, who was quickly recovering from her terrible ordeal. 'My name is Gabby Kendrick. I run the Circle K ranch with my brother Frank. We were heading back to the ranch with three prize Hereford bulls we've bought to improve the herd when this happened. I rode on ahead looking for a shallow place to cross the river. Should have noticed that patch of quicksand.'

Gabby eyed the tall stranger, waiting for a response.

'They call me . .' Then he hesitated, unsure as to which role he should be playing here. The reputation of Beavertail Bob Luman might be known in Wyoming by other than those on the wrong side of the law. Sticking to his own handle seemed the safest bet. The pause was momentary, and hidden by a cough. 'I go by the name of Drew Henry. Pleased to meet you, Miss Kendrick.'

'Make it Gabby, OK . . . Drew?' Snow-white teeth beamed back at him. 'We don't go much on formality at the Circle K.'

Drew couldn't resist a sly grin. The man's smirking regard made the winsome creature realize what a hideous apparition she must present. Those small portions of her satin features still on view visibly coloured beneath his ardent gaze. Yet to Drew's eyes she still presented a striking image.

Clawing at the sticky mess, she lurched over to the river shallows and immersed herself completely in the clear water. Thrashing around like a hooked pike, she only emerged when thoroughly satisfied that every last vestige of the odious gunge had been removed.

The change was startling.

Drew couldn't help staring at the shapely profile, now all too apparent beneath the sodden clothing. The girl's pert nose twitched, a mannerism that emphasized her freckled face.

'Some'n caught your attention, Drew?' the girl enquired, unaware of the mesmeric effect she was having on her rescuer.

The man blinked, then shook off the brief moment of ogling paralysis. He quickly looked away. Muttering some unintelligible remark, he proceeded to gather in the lariat. Then he removed his slicker from behind his mount's saddle and quickly draped it across the girl's shoulders.

'This'll keep the warmth in until you get back to

camp and dry off,' he said. 'Is it far?'

Gabby hugged the garment around herself. 'A mile back down the trail.'

Thankfully, Drew was saved from having to explain himself further by the arrival of four other riders. They paused on the edge of the river in a flurry of dust.

On witnessing a stranger seemingly in over-familiar contact with his sister, Frank Kendrick's weathered face assumed a bleak scowl. He spurred down the river bank dashing headlong across the shallows, juddering to a halt before this threatening presence. Drew couldn't help noticing the family resemblance. This guy was clearly Gabby's twin brother.

'What's goin' on here?' The snappy demand was backed up by a fistful of Remington .44. Not waiting for a reply, the Circle K boss hurried on, anxiously perceiving his sister's waterlogged appearance. 'You all right, Gabby? This guy ain't—'

'I am now,' interrupted the girl, shaking herself like a wet hound dog. Droplets of moisture from her bedraggled golden tresses sparkled in the afternoon sunlight. 'This kind stranger happened along and dragged me out of that mud hole after I'd gotten stuck.' A jutting finger pointed out the deadly patch waiting to trap the unwary. A radiant smile lit up the girl's smooth complexion. 'And it's darned lucky for me that he did.'

Drew basked in the praise lavished by this vision of loveliness.

After hearing the full explanation, Frank Kendrick put up his gun.

'OK, boys,' he shouted with a laugh. 'We found us a real live hero.' The other hands likewise holstered their weapons. Kendrick then addressed Drew. 'Much obliged to you, mister. Don't know what I'd do if anything happened to my sister. If we can help in any way, you just say the word.'

The newcomer considered the offer seriously.

'A cup of hot coffee would go down a treat.'

'Our camp's close by.' Kendrick grinned. 'And there's allus a full pot on the boil.'

'I reckon we can do a mite better'n that, Frank,' chided Gabby, while gazing raptly at her tall handsome benefactor. 'Rib-eye steak all right, Drew? With maybe some of Rooster's home-made apple pie to follow?'

'That's our crusty old cook,' supplied Frank in answer to Drew's quizzical regard.

'Just lead me to it,' glowed the good Samaritan, mounting his horse.

THREE

RUSTLERS

Following the best supper he had tasted this side of doomsday, Drew relaxed with a cigar in the pleasant company of the Circle K riders. Talk flowed back and forth. Sitting around the campfire, Drew's appreciative eye was constantly drawn to the comely female rancher whose lilting cadences slipped off the tongue like melted butter.

The subject matter was incidental until the matter of the payroll robberies was raised, One guy pointed out that they were not the only crimes being perpetrated by the gang. Rustling might not be as profitable, but it was a sight easier, due to the widespread distribution of the herds. The bigger spreads had been hit the worst as they found it impossible to maintain a constant watch on their stock. This had allowed the rustlers to operate unhindered.

'We ain't been hit so bad,' remarked Frank Kendrick. 'Being a smaller holding, we don't run enough steers to interest these varmints.'

Drew frowned. His gaze strayed to the three prize bulls, securely hobbled so that they could not stray too far.

By purchasing such magnificent beasts, Drew surmised, the Circle K harboured ambitions to move into the big time. And it was on the cards that the gang would be aware of their recent purchase. They seemed to have inside information about all matters concerning quick profits. If such were the case, trouble might well be waiting round the next bend in the trail.

When questioned, none of the hands had any notion as to whether or not the same gang was involved in the rustling.

Drew decided not to take any chances. Here was the perfect opportunity to find out. Maybe his job of foiling the Wyoming bandits would begin earlier than he'd expected.

When at last the convivial chat broke up he made his excuses for not bedding down straight away. His real purpose was to keep a weather eye open for any attempt to steal the valuable breeding animals. With only one day left before the drive reached home turf, this would be the ideal time for any rustling to be undertaken.

Drew didn't want to alarm his new acquaintances. Nor did he want them suspecting that he was anything other than a harmless drifter.

'Reckon I'll take a walk before I settle down,' he said nonchalantly. 'It helps me sleep. I'll be quiet as a mouse when I get back so as not to disturb y'all.'

In truth he had no intention of bedding down. From past experience he knew that rustlers tended to strike in the early hours, when the camp was fast asleep. But not too late, thus giving them the chance to make good their escape. Except when stampeded, cattle generally moved at a slow pace.

Settling himself behind a cluster of rocks within sight of the bulls, he knew that a long wait lay ahead. That was no hardship. He had undertaken similar stake-outs before, some lasting far longer than a single night.

He cast his mind back to earlier in the year when he had been forced to maintain a lone vigil on the hideout of Lonesome Luke Danvers. The outlaw had acquired the nickname on account of a penchant for working alone. It was not until the fifth day that the stagecoach robber had at last appeared. The broad grin creasing his bearded visage had been instantly removed by Drew's brittle challenge.

This was the first time Danvers had been caught flat-footed. And it was to be the last.

'How did you learn about this place?' he growled at the lawman who emerged from behind the log cabin. 'Nobody but me has ever been here before.'

'You should know that hard liquor loosens tongues.' Drew smiled, holding the outlaw's angry glower. 'And there's always some critter listening out for such titbits.'

'Who was it?' rasped the irate desperado, clenching his fists. 'I'll wring his scrawny neck!'

'Too late for that, Lonesome,' replied the unfazed tinstar. 'Now you just lift out them shooting irons, nice and slow. Then toss 'em over here.'

Drew's .45 never wavered an inch.

'I ain't gonna rot in no jail for the next ten years if that's what yer thinkin', mister,' blustered the outlaw, shaking his head. 'I'd sooner be stokin' the fires of Hell first.'

'That can be arranged if'n you don't surrender peaceful like.'

The smile had slipped from Drew's face as he realized that Danvers was about to draw on him.

'Don't do it, Luke,' Drew warned. 'I don't wanna kill you.'

A cold vacant cast came over the outlaw's ashen features.

He had gone beyond the point of no return. Blanching hands flexed as he slowly turned to face his adversary. Luke Danvers was not going down without a fight. Displaying the foxy manoeuvering for which he was renowned, the bandit threw himself to one side. The gun was palmed and cocked before he hit the ground.

But the lawman was ready. Three shots blasted the still air of Elkhorn Gulch. They reverberated around the enclosed clearing as Drew Henry sadly shook his head. Killing did not come easily to the loose-limbed starpacker.

With deliberate steps he approached the twitching corpse. His gun hung by his side, blue smoke twirling from the barrel.

'What a waste,' he mumbled to himself. 'Another time, another place, and you could have made something of your life.' Then a smile slowly transformed the dour aspect of his black-stubbled cheeks as he removed a dodger from his jacket pocket. 'Still. A cool grand ain't to be sniffed at, eh Luke?'

Being a Bad Boy sure had its perks. And claiming bounties on wanted felons was one such advantage. It helped boost the less than bounteous salary enjoyed by these tough law enforcers.

A silvery glow lit up the glade close to where Drew was keeping watch.

Bunches of loose cloud skimmed across the night sky, allowing a crescent moon to play a game of cat and mouse with the observant sentinel. Drew suppressed the desire for a smoke. Even the faintest glow could alert any potential felons. It was well after midnight when a movement over by the three tethered bulls caught Drew's vigilant eye.

Four men had appeared as if from nowhere. Not a sound had betrayed their presence. These guys were clearly experts in their field. While three of them were preparing to release the hobbles from each of the bulls, another had positioned himself over to the left so that he could keep an eye on the sleeping cowhands. Just in case any of them should inadvertently wake up and smell a rat.

Drew slid out from behind the rocks and cat-footed over to the guard who had his back turned. The thud of a gun butt on the side of the guy's head effectively removed one of the rustlers from the action. The unconscious rustler crumpled soundlessly to the ground.

Drew now turned his attention to the three remaining outlaws. Unaware of the fate meted out to their buddy, the gang continued with their efforts to release the bulls.

Drew sucked in a deep breath.

Tackling these varmints called for a more robust approach. He drew both revolvers and thumbed back the hammers. The double clicks of the cocking six-shooters cut through the silence of the night. It was a sound that instantly registered in the minds of all men who lived by the gun.

'The game's up, boys,' he hollered loud enough to awaken the slumbering ranch hands. 'Throw down your weapons and surrender.'

But these critters were no greenhorn desperadoes. Muttered imprecations from the roused herders were drowned out by the blast of firearms from the rustlers. All hell had broken loose. Lancing tongues of orange flame spat from three revolvers. They were aimed in the general direction of the threatening challenge to their sneaking thievery.

Drew bobbed down out of the firing line.

'We've been rumbled,' shouted a tremulous voice.

Drew cursed. He hadn't reckoned with the gang's alertness to a warning of capture. It was in his nature always to offer culprits the chance to give themselves up and thus avoid any shooting. Maybe cutting loose with his guns would have been more decisive. Too late for that now.

The moon's taking the decision at that precise moment to disappear behind a roving cloudbank hadn't done him any favours either.

'Let's get outa here!'

Three blurred shadows dashed across the open ground to the waiting horses, guns still blazing.

'What in tarnation is goin' on?'

Frank Kendrick had stumbled into the light cast by the still glowing embers of the campfire. His black silhouette made a perfect target.

'Keep your head down!' yelled Drew as he return the fire of the rustlers.

But this only served to concentrate their aim. A loose bullet lifted his hat, scoring a thin furrow across the top of his head. With a sharp cry of pain the lawman dropped to his knees. No more than a scalp wound, it was enough to stall his pursuit of the fleeing cattle-thieves.

A terrified bawling from the panicking bulls mingled with the discordant shouts and yells from the roused cowpokes. Scared witless, the large animals thrashed about. Hoofs pounded the earth as they desperately tried to free themselves. But the hobbles frustrated their struggles.

Sufficient turmoil was created, however, to cover the ignominious flight of the thwarted rustlers. Drumming hoofs quickly faded into the inky blackness as they disappeared.

Guns drawn, but too late for the action, Frank and the other hands hurried over. The rancher's first concern was to check on his valuable stock. Gabby's solicitude was for the fallen man who had saved them from being stolen.

'Help me get him over to the fire,' she said to one of the cowboys. 'Let's see how bad this wound is.'

'Take care . . . of that . . . jasper first,' gasped Drew, pointing to the still unconscious form of the downed rustler.

'Arkansas!' she called across to a nearby hand. 'Get this varmint tied up good so's he can't get away.'

'Sure thing, Gabby,' replied the cowpoke known as Arkansas Charley. He stumped over to the fallen outlaw, unceremoniously booting the prone figure in the ribs. A hoarse groan informed him that the critter was coming round. 'You've got some questions to answer, mister,' he rasped while securing the man with his lariat.

It was another half-hour before the camp settled down. The bulls had been calmed, the fire rekindled, and some coffee brewed as the events of the night were replayed. All thoughts of sleep had been thrust aside. Three cowboys were put on guard in case the rustlers decided to try again. Unlikely, but Frank Kendrick was taking no chances.

'It's only three hours until dawn,' he said. 'We'll pull out at first light. No sense hangin' around. Sooner we get these big fellas back to the ranch the better I'll feel.'

He moved away to check on the animals once again.

Drew sat by the fire, pulling on a cigar. He was feeling downcast. What sort of special agent was it who allowed a bunch of no-good rustlers to turn the tables on him? The more he thought about it, the more convinced he became that these skunks were no ordinary bunch of desperadoes. Perched on a nearby cottonwood, an owl hooted in sympathy.

Could be they were the notorious Starrbreakers.

He was now able fully to comprehend why the Bureau had been given the job of removing these villains from Wyoming territory. But at least one positive element had emerged from this fiasco. One of the critters had been captured.

Drew threw a vitriolic glare towards the pinioned captive. It was time to discover the truth behind the mysterious gang that was panicking the authorities. He stood up and gestured for Frank to follow him over to where the Mexican was tied to a tree.

'Time for some talking, mister,' snapped the special agent, standing over the doleful rustler. 'Who's your boss, and where do your buddies hang out?'

The Mexican looked at them with puzzlement etched across his swarthy fat face. '*No entiendo, señors,*' he whined shaking his head. '*Lopez no hablo el inglés.*'

'What's the damned greaser mumblin' about?' rasped Kendrick acidly.

'Sounds to me like he don't speak the lingo,' replied Drew.

The rancher spat out a lurid epithet, then grabbed a hold of the man's lank black hair and shook him roughly like a dog with a rabbit. 'Don't give me that, scumbag,' he hollered snatching his gun out and jamming the barrel up the quaking rustler's pudgy snout. 'You're just stallin'. Now sing, damn you, or I'll poison that heathen heart with hot lead.'

Even if he couldn't understand English, the prisoner was well aware of the threat now posed to life and limb. A flurry of garbled words poured forth in his own tongue. It was only a swift backhander from Kendrick that stanched the flow.

'Anybody here speak Mex?' the ranch boss enquired of the other hands. Nobody spoke. 'Then there's only one way to find out if this jigger is tellin' the truth.' He turned to address a stocky cowpoke who was hovering close by. 'Over here, Razor!'

Ben Sharp ambled across and gave his boss a puzzled look. The bow-legged cowboy had earned his moniker on account of his expertise with a knife when gelding horses and cattle. Thus far his skills had not been practised on humans. That omission might soon be remedied.

Kendrick responded with an amiable smile and a sly wink hidden from the Mexican's anxious gaze. Then he spoke in a deliberately casual tone.

'You're the best guy I ever saw with a knife, Razor.' Sharp deftly removed the said implement and flicked open the folded blade. Smirking at the gaping captive, he tossed the deadly weapon into the air with his right hand and caught it with his left. Light from the fire glinted on the shiny steel. Then he snapped it shut, slipping it back into his jeans. 'Go to work on this skunk. Let's see if it's right what I read in a book.'

'And what might that be, boss?'

'It said that castrated prisoners who have their balls removed always speak in a high voice for ever after.' The two cowpokes continued talking in a friendly manner, as they would over a couple of beers. 'You reckon it'll take long to slice off this fella's privates?' asked Kendrick.

'Depends on how tough the skin is,' replied Sharp with nonchalant ease. He was thoroughly enjoying the subterfuge. 'Usually, it would take only a few quick cuts. And hey presto! They're off. Might be a heap of blood though. And the slimy greaser won't be sitting a horse for some time.'

'Not to mention having his way with the calico queens.'

The two punchers laughed at the notion.

The Mexican remained nonplussed. He continued to look uneasy, but no more so than previously. The threat to his manhood would have surely resulted in a far more vociferous reaction had he been aware of the meaning of the dialogue. Clearly he had not understood. And that meant he was telling the truth concerning his ignorance of English.

The jovial smirk disappeared from Kendrick's face. Then he uttered a mournful sigh.

'OK, Ben, get back to work. This jasper ain't able to spill the beans. At least nothing that we can understand.'

Both men wandered away, shoulders hunched, leaving the prisoner more baffled than ever.

Drew sat down and poured a mug of coffee with four spoonsful of sugar. He needed the boost. Getting to grips with this gang was going to be tougher than he had hoped. It was Gabby Kendrick who broke into his gloomy reflections.

'You shouldn't have tackled that bunch on your ownsome,' she chided the bandaged saviour of their herd. A white strip of cloth swathed his head. It was stained red where blood was seeping through. 'You'll need to get that gash fixed properly by the doc when you reach Kaycee.'

Drew smiled as she dexterously adjusted the covering. He was enjoying the attention from this enchanting angel.

'You seem to have done a pretty good job of patching me up.' He peered at his image in a mirror, glowing under the girl's disarming gaze. 'Makes me look like an old pirate.'

The light-hearted banter was cut short by Gabby's brother calling the hands to rouse up and hit the trail.

'Maybe you would consider staying on after we've delivered the prisoner to the sheriff at Casper?'

The enquiry caught Drew off balance. He was taken aback by the unexpected proposal. In the light of his current assignment, it was the last thing he wanted. He affected a pained expression to cover his dilemma. As Gabby fussed around like a mother hen, it afforded him chance to figure out a suitable excuse for turning her down.

'Don't reckon I'd make a good cowpoke,' he voiced somewhat reluctantly. In truth, he would have dearly relished spending more time in Gabby's company. Perhaps when this business had been brought to a satisfactory conclusion, he could take her up on it.

'How's that, Drew?' enquired Gabby. 'I thought you were hoping to get work at the KC ranch.' Her mouth dipped in a sad pout. The lowered chin produced a sorrowful expression. 'Me and Frank have talked it over. We were gonna offer you a job on our spread. Not as big as the KC, but a heap friendlier.'

'That's mighty kind of you folks,' Drew muttered, somewhat abashed. He had to think quickly of a suitable excuse. 'But my game is buying and selling. I'm basically a loner. Don't operate too well in a group.'

'You seem to have done OK so far,' muttered Frank doubtfully.

'Rescuing your sister, then helping to foil the rustlers don't count.' Drew underscored the remark with a firm squaring of the shoulders. 'Any man worth his salt would have done the same.' He shrugged. 'Anyways, I've got a meeting with some buyers in Kaycee that can't be postponed. I'll stick around until this varmint is jailed at Casper, then we'll have to part company.'

'So we won't be seeing you again?' Gabby's sorrowful plea brought a lump to the agent's throat making him feel like a real killjoy. The label of Bad Boy seemed to fit him like a glove.

'Didn't say that,' urged Drew anxiously, trying to backtrack. 'When my business is finished, I'll sure try to look you up.' A wry grin broke across the chiselled features. 'And if'n that offer's still open, then who knows?'

FOUR

INCIDENT AT KAYCEE

The Circle K hands, accompanied by Drew Henry, had broken camp before sunup. Any sleep forfeited due to the failed attempt to steal the prize bulls could be made up on the trail. By mid-morning they were nearing the Sweetwater which was where the lawman bid them farewell.

'You make sure to come visit with us once your business is done in Kaycee,' prompted Frank Kendrick. 'That offer of a job still stands.'

'I'll sure keep it mind,' replied Drew, although he was loath to commit himself. 'Depends if I get a better offer.' He laughed, trying to brush off the notion of any committment on his part.

With a brief wave he disappeared over a low knoll, hauling the prisoner in his wake.

Frank sensed that his sister was more than a touch melancholic at her saviour's departure. But he held his peace, convinced she would soon get over it. After all, they had only known the guy for one day.

'You ride ahead, sis,' he called from the far side of the strung-out line of riders. 'Check for a shallow crossing of the river. And keep your eyes peeled for them rustlers.' As she swung her mount towards the line of willows marking the river's meandering course, Frank added with a brisk guffaw, 'And this time, watch out for any mud holes waiting to grab you out of the saddle. Next time there might not be a handsome knight riding past to save you.'

Gabby responded with a tight-lipped nod of the head before spurring off.

Two days of steady riding passed before Drew came in sight of the cluster of buildings that comprised the town of Kaycee. Nobody knew him here. Not even the local tinstar.

His boss, Isaac Thruxton, had deemed it prudent that the two law officers should not meet during the powwow at Laramie. With the special agent assuming the guise of an escaped outlaw, the role could best be played out with Ramsey in total ignorance as to his real identity. That way no slip-ups would be made.

Jogging up the main street, Drew pulled his hat down low. His searching eyes panned the array of clapboard structures. Nobody paid him any heed. Then he saw it. A sign advertising Heck Ramsey: County Sheriff, swung in the gentle breeze. And there lazing in the shade of the veranda was the man himself.

Drew's weathered features cracked in a smile.

The guy's mouth was hanging open. He was clearly enjoying a doze in the early afternoon sun. Grey streaks in the black moustache and an over-generous girth indicated that Ramsey was not in the first flush of youth. But Drew was well aware of the solid reputation he had acquired as a dependable lawman over the years. In consequence, he had no intention of taking this ostensibly torpid persona for granted.

A slight shift of the lawman's hat proved the point. The newcomer had been eyeballed. Otherwise the apparently slumbering lawdog remained idle.

Drew hauled up in front of the Bee Hive saloon. Had he chanced to look up, he would have clapped eyes on the principal object of his mission.

Leroy Starr angled a casual peeper towards the stranger tying up below. Just another drifter passing through. The gang leader took another slug of the special reserve whisky that Belle kept for visiting dignitaries. His thoughts were elsewhere. Tensed up and on edge, he was not looking forward to the inevitable tongue-lashing that would result when Belle learnt of the failed attempt to rustle the Circle K bulls.

The click of high heels in the outer corridor told him that the boss had arrived. Starr brushed away the thin film of sweat coating his brow. Sashaying through the door came Belle, the heavy material of her long dress rustling like fallen leaves. Leroy could not help but ogle the woman. He was scared of no man. But the outlaw queen was something else.

As soon as Belle observed the bottle in Starr's hand she suspected that all was not well. A scowl clouded the heavily rouged cheeks.

'Did you get them?'

The waspish question stymied the outlaw. His mouth hung open as he figured out how best to relate the events of the failed mission. He took another swig, coughing as the raw spirit hit the back of his throat.

'Well, Leroy?' the feisty woman repeated in a low yet menacing tone while assuming a hectoring stance. 'Them prized bulls. Are they safely hidden?'

'Things ... didn't quite work out as we'd planned,' Starr gulped hesitantly. 'Kendrick must have suspected that some'n was in the air. And he had a guard posted.'

A rabid hiss issued from between the woman's gritted teeth. This was not what she wanted to hear.

'You're telling me that the great Leroy Starr allowed a greenhorn outfit like the Circle K to outwit him?' The ridicule was laced with a heavy dose of acid. Belle shook her head angrily. The red tresses shuddered like a rampant blaze of fire. 'So what went wrong?'

Starr shrugged. 'One of 'em slugged Lopez then called on us to surrender. It was a set-up. I can't figure how some hick cowpoke got the better of Lopez. D'yuh think they might have hired a gunfighter?'

Belle ignored the question.

'What about Lopez?' Concern about having the law sniffing round was etched on her face. 'Will he talk?'

'Not a chance,' scoffed Starr, regaining his former bravado. 'The greaser might be a lethal gunhand, but he's illiterate. Can't string two words together. So don't you fret none. Anyway, there'll be other capers,' he said, laying an arm around her shoulder. 'It's just a temporary setback. And it won't affect us, will it?'

Belle stamped her feet, angrily pushing off the attempted embrace. 'How many times do I have to say it, lunkhead? There ain't no *us*. This is a business partnership. And that's all.' She didn't wait for any show of remonstration, turning her back on the grimacing outlaw. 'Now get back to the cabin. There's another job I've got planned. And this time, make sure there ain't no slip-ups, savvy? I'll come out there after the saloon closes.'

'S-sure thing, Belle,' the browbeaten outlaw mumbled. 'You're the boss.'

'And don't you forget it!'

He left by the back stairway to avoid being spotted by any prying eyes.

Meanwhile, out front Drew Henry was just entering the Bee Hive. And like many others before him, he couldn't resist a chuckle at the poetic lyrics inviting drinkers to sample the wares on offer within. He pushed through the doors and ambled over to the bar.

'What's yer poison, stranger,' enquired a stick-thin

bartender whose black hair was plastered to his scalp with evil-smelling pomade.

Drew sniffed. Now was the time to get into his tough-guy stance. From here on, he had to adopt the air of the cocky desperado recently escaped from jail. Beavertail Bob Luman was in business.

'Anything that'll get the stink of rancid hair tonic outa my nose.'

Jess McCafferty angled a caustic glower at the newcomer.

'Ain't no need for insults, fella,' he snapped. 'We don't take kindly to that sort of talk in the Bee Hive.'

A snap of the fingers brought three lounging drinkers suddenly to life. The hardcases had been hidden from view round the far corner of the bar. Scraping chairs found them on their feet, hands reaching for holstered pistols ready to meet the challenge of this insolent drifter.

Suddenly, the threat of gunplay was suspended.

'Hold it, boys!' The cutting interjection came from the ornate staircase at the far end of the room. 'This fella does have a point, Jess,' suggested a husky voice that purred with effortless ease from the feline temptress. 'You have been laying it on bit thick of late.'

The hired help chuckled. McCafferty threw them a baleful glare, huffed some while mentally preening his ruffled feathers. But he kept silent, considering it judicious to accept the woman's rebuke.

Drew swung on his heel to face the source of the dulcet tones. His eyes widened perceptibly at the sight of the green goddess now swaying provocatively as she glided across the floor of the saloon to stand before him. The crowd of onlookers parted to let her through.

'Give the man a drink . . . on the house,' she said holding the stranger's concentrated stare as the barman slid a beer across the shiny surface. Drew took a sip. The woman held out a small hand while appraising the tall stranger. 'The name's Belle Sherman. I own the Bee Hive.'

Drew accepted the proferred palm.

'Bob Luman,' he replied, coughing out the name with a slight croak. 'Beavertail to my friends. I used to do some trapping.' He casually flicked the small flat cubtail affixed to his hatband. 'But then I figured that trapping other folks' dough was a lot easier. It pays better too.'

Playing the role of an escaped convict felt strange. So far he had given nothing away. Just a gentle hint. But he slotted into the deception with confident ease. A libertine smile edged aside the surprise of seconds before. With a practised flourish, he removed his hat and performed a discreet bow.

'And I hope such a delectable portrait as yourself, Miss Sherman, will choose to join that select group of *amigos*.'

Belle's emerald eyes flashed.

Taking a step back, hands resting on her curvy hips, she coolly studied this precocious rooster. He had nerve, that was for darned sure. And there was no denying that he was a handsome devil, a cut above the normal standard of clientele who frequented the saloon. But Belle Sherman had no intention of succumbing to unctuous flattery from any man.

'Think a lot of yourself, don't you, *Mister* Luman?' she sneered, deliberately emphasizing the title. Bob's response was to raise a languid eyebrow. 'Well, this gal don't jump through hoops for nobody, least of all for some cheapskate's oily tune. . . .'

Luman placed a finger over the wide mouth, instantly stilling the impassioned tirade. Without speaking he pulled the woman close and kissed her fervently on the lips. Belle was caught completely off guard. For a brief moment she succumbed to the amorous gesture.

Then reality bit deep. Nobody acted in such a brazen manner with Belle Sherman. Exhibiting a forceful display of her own, she pushed him away, the flat of her hand lashing out across the offender's cheek. The resounding slap could be clearly heard throughout the room. But the recipient merely curled his lip into an arrogant smirk. His response was a curt bow.

'My apologies, madam, if I offended you,' he said. 'But such delectable lips deserve to be' – he paused offering the woman an enticing smile before adding – 'trapped by mine.'

Belle was left speechless. Aiming a final look of disdain at this impudent stranger, she turn about and flounced off back up the staircase to her apartment. Bob's lustful gaze pursued her until she had disappeared from view. He failed to see the look of similar appetite that she gave him from behind a curtain.

Belle's hand strayed to her red lips. This was a new and exciting experience. Her hands were shaking. Her whole body trembled from the shock. Stumbling into her room, she grabbed hold of the abandoned whisky bottle, splashed a double measure into a glass and sank it in a single draught. If nothing else, the hard liquor helped to calm her pounding heart.

Beavertail Bob Luman! Was he the one for whom she had been seeking? It barely seemed possible.

A year after arriving in Kaycee, Belle had been seriously considering her future. No longer in the first flush of youth, she now wanted out of this game. Constantly on her guard, the so-called outlaw queen was finding it ever more difficult to maintain the outward appearance of a respectable, somewhat aloof businesswoman.

Mixing with hard-boiled rannies like Leroy Starr was no picnic. The guy was becoming a tiresome jerk.

Like any normal female, Belle Sherman craved the normality of settling down with a real man and enjoying a family life. She had built up a sizeable poke, which was now resting in a Denver bank vault. But shucking her owlhoot ways was much harder said than done. Until a suitable opportunity arose, she would have to stick with the tough persona that had been diligently constructed as a means of survival in a man's world.

Entering her boudoir, Belle threw off her clothes and stepped into the hot bath prepared by her personal maid. The need to settle jangling nerves overrode all other considerations at that moment.

Indeed, so confused were the outlaw queen's thoughts that she failed to heed the unrestrained guffaw from Jess McCafferty that followed her showy departure.

'Seems like you upset the boss, mister,' snarled the barkeep. 'And that ain't nice. We've got ways of dealing with skunks that don't know how to behave in front of a lady, ain't we boys?'

A series of concurring grunts greeted the barman's threatening harangue.

Luman backed away towards his end of the bar. Loosening the twin Colts in their holsters, he watched eagle-eyed as the three gunmen ranged themselves across the far end of the room. Three to one was not good odds, even for a shootist of Drew Henry's capability.

The tension in the room was palpable. All knew that a gunfight was imminent. As one, chairs slammed back, the crowd surging like a tidal wave towards the door. Within seconds the saloon was empty. Even Jess McCafferty had thought it wise to vacate his post behind the bar.

Bob Luman ducked down behind the overhanging bar top and cast a wary peeper down the narrow passage behind. What he saw brought a smile to his face.

Maybe the odds could now be stacked in his favour after all. A shotgun lay resting on a shelf. McCafferty's answer to bad payers and troublemakers.

A flurry of shots rang out. Chunks of mahogany flew past the head of the concealed gunman.

'Where is he?' sang out an alarmed voice.

'Over behind the bar,' came back the shaky reply.

The shooting eased off as the attackers considered how best to deal with their quarry. Luman took the opportunity of reminding them that it would be no simple exercise. Sticking a head round the side of the bar, he rapidly snapped off a couple of shots. They were not meant to strike home, merely to engender a degree of respect.

Luman needed time. Scuttling on all fours down to the far end of the bar, he grabbed the shotgun en route. Both hammers clicked back.

'You take that end, Mace,' directed a gruff voice. 'I'll catch him if'n he tries to come out this end.'

'Sure thing, Bucky.'

A scuffling of boot leather informed Luman that he had very little time to avoid being caught in cross-fire. Judging where the voice had come from, he sucked in a deep breath.

Another short second passed. Then he sprang to his feet and let fly with both barrels. The huge blast stung his ears as it echoed round the bare wooden walls of the saloon. Black powder smoke spewed forth. Without waiting to observe whether the double charge had struck home, he ducked back down again.

He need not have worried. A choking gurgle informed him that one gunman was out of the frame.

'Bucky's been hit!' yelped Hawk Wagoner.

The cry was edged with panic as the remaining two hardcases realized that, with their leader down, this varmint was a serious threat to their continued good health. But hard-boiled gunmen are at their most dangerous when under pressure. And Luman knew that reserves would likely be arriving at any minute. A supposition that was confirmed by Mace Fargo.

'Then keep yer head down and sit tight,' he returned in a brittle tone. 'All this shootin' will bring the boss to our aid. This turkey ain't goin' nowhere.'

Fargo's confident manner bolstered his confederate's wilting nerve. 'I've gotten this end of the bar covered,' replied Wagoner confidently.

Raising his voice, Fargo snapped a brusque reminder to the object of their attack that there would be no quarter given in the lethal exchange. 'Hear that, mister! The only way you'll be leavin' the Bee Hive is in a pine box. Bucky Hayes was a good buddy of ours.'

The menacing threat was supported by another blast of gunfire.

Luman knew that he would have to get out soon, or go down in a hail of bullets. But how?

There was only one way out of this rattler's nest.

A stool used by the barman was the answer. Leathering his guns, Luman hefted the stool. Head lowered, he edged along behind the bar back towards the front of the saloon, where he braced himself for the challenge. A single mighty heave and the stool hurtled through the window.

Glass flew in all directions.

Without pausing to ascertain the situation of his adversaries, Luman followed immediately behind. A perfectly arched dive, head first, took him through the ragged hole on to the sidewalk, where he landed with a bump.

The sudden bid for freedom had caught the saloon toughs on the wrong foot. But they quickly recovered. Gunfire pursued the fugitive through the gap knocking out glass fragments still clinging to the window frame. Jagged slivers plucked at Luman's clothes, one shard opening up a flap of skin on his cheek. The sudden pain went unheeded as the bogus desperado quickly regained his feet, only to be confronted by a new threat.

'What's all the ruckus about?' The voice of Heck Ramsey snapped out a terse challenge. The sheriff had his gun drawn. 'In town for less than an hour and you're causing more trouble than a rabid cur.' The lawman grabbed Luman's arm while tickling his spine with the revolver. 'You're under arrest for disturbing the peace.'

But having escaped from one tight corner, Luman did not intend to surrender willingly. He had work to do and getting thrown into jail was not going to help him rid the territory of its criminal element.

Slamming his elbow into the sheriff's midriff, he pivoted on his left boot and continued the counter-attack. The stiff palm of his hand slammed down on to the sheriff's arm. Ramsey emitted a grunt of pain, doubling up as an elbow jabbed his stomach. A rush of displaced air hissed through clenched teeth.

Instinctively he pulled the trigger and his gun went off. But the bullet ploughed harmlessly into the sidewalk.

Unthinking, Luman then powered a solid right hook to the exposed jaw of the tottering lawdog. The poor sucker hit the ground like a sack of potatoes.

Angry voices intent on revenge informed the fugitive that he was not out of danger yet. He hit the saddle on the run and galloped out of town. Zipping volleys of hot lead buzzed around his lowered head like angry hornets. Townsfolk attempting to cross the street were scattered like chaff in the wind. Hound dogs yapped but held back lest they be trampled underfoot.

Spurring down the first alleyway, he urged his mount to lengthen its stride. In a matter of minutes he had left the huddle of buildings behind. A good half-hour passed before he slowed the lathered grey to an easy canter.

'Well done, Snapper!' He praised the sweating horse, rubbing her ears affectionately. 'That showed them critters that Beavertail Bob ain't gonna be pushed around by nobody.'

Now that he had time to reflect on the startling episode, he reckoned that it had done his cause no harm whatsoever. Indeed, the bogus outlaw had presented his credentials in the best possible manner. It could only serve to enhance his chances of being accepted by the Starrbreakers. All he had to do now was find out where they were holed up and introduce himself.

A frown clouded the tanned features. The euphoria of a few seconds before faded like the evening sunset. He regretted having had to manhandle the ageing sheriff. It had been a necessity and he hoped the old guy had escaped with nothing more than a stiff jaw.

Then another thought struck home. How was he going to make himself known to the gang? They had always disappeared into thin air following a heist. And no law officer ever had the slightest notion of how to flush them out. Could one man really hope to accomplish what many had dismally failed to do?

He shrugged off the threatening despondency. That was why the boss had chosen him, because he had sound faith in Drew Henry's ability to search out and defeat this challenge to law and order.

Back straight, head held high, the stolid expression on his face exuded a firm determination to succeed in his task. The only clue he had been given was that the gang had always headed west towards the Big Horn Mountains. Successful outlaw gangs tended to have lookouts guarding all access points to their secret hideaways.

By riding the same trail, he hoped that eventually someone would spot him and pass the word.

FIVE

HOLE IN THE WALL

For two days Luman pointed his horse across the rolling grassland. Fractured turrets of red sandstone reared up to block his path. But there was no way through the impregnable barrier. Retracing his steps along the base of the scree-choked wall of cliffs, he had seen nothing that even slightly resembled a hole. Walls of rock there were in profusion.

On the third day, with his provisions running low, he encountered a rift that had been hidden from view.

A canyon, hemmed in by vertical crags, was made all the more sinister by dark shadowy recesses where little light could penetrate. His heart raced. Could this be the legendary Hole? Emerging at the far end, his heart sank as he was met by more of the same. Mighty mesas with narrow cracks turned out to be impenetrable box canyons when explored.

Elation at having beaten the puzzle gave way to disenchantment.

Time was running out. He was down to chewing on strips of jerked beef. The spurious escaped convict was getting nervy. Concern was being edged out by fear that he could end up feeding the critters that resided in this bizarre labyrinth. Nobody would ever discover what happened to Drew Henry, special agent and Bad Boy. Bleached white by aeons of sun and rain, his bones would eventually crumble to dust.

Luman tried to shake off the depression flooding his brain. While he still had breath in his body, there was hope.

Then he felt it.

That itchy feeling at the aback of his neck. The sixth sense that had always served him well since he'd first pinned on a tin star. At last. His plan to infiltrate the indomitable hideout had paid dividends.

Someone had him under surveillance. It had to be one of the gang, an outer sentinel. A double hoot followed, akin to the call of a cactus wren, but of human origin. A prearranged signal?

His body tensed as he slowed his mount to a walk. Any sign of panic could mean a bullet in the back. Ten minutes later, two guards rode out from behind a clutch of boulders, one on either side of the ravine. Each had a rifle at his shoulder. And they were pointed straight at Luman's head.

'Hold it right there, mister,' came the blunt command from the one on the left. A short stumpy jasper called Bitter Creek Watson.

'And get them hands up, pronto!' Another gruff order, this time from Rusty Laverne, who had been trailing behind.

Luman complied. He had no intention of jeopardizing his hard-won chance to become an accepted member of the Starrbreakers.

'So who are you, fella?' said the taller man, sporting a flowing black moustache nudging his mount forward. 'Give me one cast-iron reason why we shouldn't drill you here and now. And it better be good.'

Luman hesitated. Suddenly confronted by these mean-eyed desperadoes in the bleak wilderness demanded a kid-glove approach. So he needed to pick his next words carefully if he wanted to remain healthy.

The cocky red-headed kid took this for a sign of guilt.

'You heard the man, dummy. Out with it or you'll be gettin' a taste of Judge Henry here.'

Drew couldn't resist a brief smile at the innocent analogy.

Laverne waved his rifle, uttering a manic honk of derision. He was eager for some action. Being one of the new boys, Rusty had been given the irksome task of first lookout. This was his second day stuck on the ridge overlooking the main access to the Hole. And the arrival of an interloper was a welcome relief from the boredom.

'And what you doin' trespassin' on private land?'

'The name's Bob Luman,' replied the newcomer,

smiling at the notion that the Hole in the Wall was owner-occupied by a bunch of outlaws. Nevertheless, he recognized that the kid was no tenderfoot and kept his hands well clear of the hardware. A cold regard locked on to the strutting peacock. 'Some folks call me Beavertail.'

Laverne shrugged. Being an outlaw from the northern territory of Montana, the young tearaway was not acquainted with Luman's reputation.

'Don't mean nothin' to me.' He ratcheted back the lever of his carbine. 'What say we get rid of this dude, Bitter Creek?'

But Watson was a New Mexico desperado and fully aware of the sizeable bounty the outlaw had acquired for his skulduggery down south. It was also common knowledge that Bob Luman was serving a ten stretch in the Colorado pen. So what was he doing in Wyoming?

Watson leaned forward over the neck of his horse. A cold regard locked on to the intruder. Then he posed the obvious question. 'Heard tell that Beavertail Bob was serving time in Denver.' The Starrbreaker's baleful gaze narrowed with suspicion, his voice assuming a hint of menace. 'So what you doin' in these parts?'

Luman had his fictional narrative ready. 'I escaped from a chain gang last month. Had some of the cons stage a fight to draw off the guards. Life down that way was gettin' too hot.' He paused, gestured whether a smoke was OK. After getting the nod from Watson, he went on: 'So I figured to start up again in

Wyoming. The word had come down the grapevine that a gang known as the Starrbreakers were making fools of the local lawdogs.'

Watson liked that and joined in the hearty chortling. 'You ain't wrong there, Bob. We've gotten the territory sewn up tight as a drumskin.' A lone coyote howled its own accordance with the outlaw's assertion.

'So I was hopin' that the boss might feel the need of an extra hand,' Luman said, with a nonchalant lift of his shoulders. 'What d'yuh reckon, boys?'

Watson expressed full agreement with the suggestion. 'A guy of your rep should have no problem persuading Leroy to put you on the payroll.' He laughed as a thought occurred. 'That is, when we next take one.'

Chuckles all round again.

'So where in tarnation is this Hole in the Wall that's got the law so all-fired up?' queried Luman, stressing his amazement at the gang's mystifying way of disappearing after every robbery.

Laverne jumped in, jabbing a finger towards the shattered wall of rock facing them on the far side of enclosed amphitheare.

'Cain't yuh see it, Beavertail?' he gushed with glee. 'Sticks out like a whore's front line.'

Luman followed the direction indicated, but all he could see was an insuperable red stronghold of cliffs. He was nonplussed.

'That's why the Starrbreakers ain't never been busted,' smirked Watson, kneeing his horse towards the rocky phalanx. 'Come on. I'll show yuh.' Before setting off, Watson turned to his partner and said, 'You stay here, Rusty. Just in case this jigger is scouting the lie of the land for a posse.'

'Sure thing, Creek,' replied Laverne. He resumed his sentry watch.

As the two riders approached the apparently solid wall, a thin track took shape. Stony and quite steep, it meandered up the fractured rubble of the cliffs, twisting and winding as it followed the layered beds of rock. Barely more than six feet wide, the riders were forced down to single file. A buzzard perched on a tree stump emitted a mournful caw as the two riders passed beneath its precarious roost.

Higher and higher they climbed until at last they breasted the upper mesa. Suddenly, an expansive panorama opened out.

The gradient on the far side was much easier on the horses. After the initial descent around boulders that were taller than a church steeple, they picked up to a steady canter down a shallow grass slope. Before them, the broad valley of Buffalo Creek stretched away unbroken to the horizon.

'Yehaaar!' hollered Bitter Creek Watson. 'Now ain't that some'n?'

Luman was awestruck, almost struck dumb, by the bewildering sight that greeted his bulging orbs.

'There sure ain't no denyin' that,' he declared, gaping open-mouthed at the herds of cattle held in the secret enclave. 'No wonder you guys have it all your own way. I sure am impressed and that's a fact.'

Together they galloped down the grade towards the distant cluster of log buildings that was home to the Starrbreakers.

The approaching riders had been spotted well before they reined up outside the log cabin. One man stood on the veranda out front, leaning against the doorjamb. A double-barrelled Greener nestled casually in his arms, presenting the image that he hadn't a care in the world.

But Luman was not fooled. He had also noted that three other gun barrels were aimed in his direction from strategic places of concealment. These boys sure don't take chances, mused the newcomer.

'Its OK, Leroy!' shouted Watson. 'We found this jasper wandering around the badlands east of the Roughnecks. Reckons he wants to join up.'

'Does he now?' purred the gang leader, arrowing a malignant glower chock-full of hellfire at the stranger. 'And why should we do that?'

'Claims that he's escaped from the Colorado pen and the pickin's are rather lean down south,' replied Watson.

'I don't allow any ol' gunslinger into my gang, mister,' snarled Starr, levering himself off the door-post and swinging the shotgun to cover the seated rider. 'You best have a darned sight better reason than that for stickin' your butt in my affairs.' The challenge was accompanied by a double click.

Like two prize fighters waying up their chances, the duo stared each other out, neither willing to give way.

It was Luman who deemed it prudent to puncture the pregnant silence.

'The name Beavertail Bob Luman meaning anything to you?'

The question brought Starr up short. His eyes bulged. Suddenly his whole demeanour changed, the starchy persona palpably relaxing. He laid the shotgun aside and stepped down.

'Why didn't you say, Bob?' warbled the gang leader, now all smiles and *bonhomie*. 'I coulda blasted you into the hereafter.' He stuck out a hand. 'Be more'n glad to have you join the gang. Ain't no denyin' that we could use a guy with your credentials to strengthen our grip on the territory.' Luman accepted the plaudit with mellowed restraint. 'Come inside and we can talk over a bottle of premium-grade Scotch.'

'I could sure use a snort after wandering around like a blind man in them canyons,' concurred Luman stepping down. 'You sure got one dandy hideout here. No wonder them crazy lawdogs are running themselves ragged chasin' around in circles.'

'And disappearin' up their own asses,' added a hardcase by the name of Vic Stride, with a hearty guffaw.

For the next two hours the two men swapped anecdotes, each trying to outdo the other with ever more lurid accounts of derring-do. It was all friendly stuff. The Bad Boy had committed to memory a whole file of Bob Luman exploits. Nevertheless, he couldn't resist adding a few touches of his own to impress Starr.

'There was that time down in Cimarron,' he recollected, accepting one of Starr's special Havana cigars. He nodded in appreciation before continuing: 'Jake Monday and his gang figured on taking the town apart following a failed attempt to rob the Denver-Rio Grande railroad. I was running the Aqua Fria saloon at the time. No way was I gonna let them goofballs wreck my joint.'

Starr was all ears. 'What did yuh do, Bob?' he asked eagerly, cheeks red and blotched with the hard liquor. Luman was more wily, giving the impression that he was more drunk than was indeed the case.

'I didn't wait for them to invade my place. Instead, I loaded up a cut-down Greener.' He aimed a pointed gaze at the Greener holding centre stage above the big stone fireplace. Starr acknowledged the choice of weapon as his new sidekick added with a conspiratorial wink. 'Then I went hunting.'

Luman paused, drawing hard on another prized Havana.

'Yeah! Yeah!' urged the excited gang boss.

'I waited in the middle of the street until Monday emerged from the Palace bar. He was all liquored up and never saw me. "You Jake Monday?" I called over. "Who wants to know?" he slurred. "The guy who's mailing a cartridge with your name on it." Then I blasted him straight through a butcher's window. With their leader gone, the others were like headless chickens. Disappeared like the desert wind.'

Luman finished the tale with a ribald chuckle. 'And can you believe it? The town marshal even paid me a reward for downing the guy.'

The Bad Boy settled a caustic peeper on to his new partner. The guy was bleary-eyed and ready to keel over. Luman judged it time to do a bit of digging. Likely Starr wouldn't recall any of it in the morning.

'You the big cheese of this outfit then, Leroy?' enquired Luman pushing the second bottle of Scotch towards Starr's searching hand.

'Darned right I am,' Leroy snapped, trying to square his ruffled shoulders but falling back as his flaccid muscles gave way. 'The boys are under my control when we pull jobs.'

'And you organize everything?'

'Well. . . .' Starr drawled, his mouth twisting. 'I have to agree to all the plans that the boss has worked out. No heists go ahead without the say-so of Leroy Starr.' He jabbed a thumb at his chest.

Luman's eyes widened. So there was a Mr Big, who was the real brains behind this set-up. That was something the Bureau hadn't reckoned with. So now came the big question.

'And who is that, then?'

Starr was drunk, but not that far gone. He tapped his nose in a sly manner. 'You'll find out tomorrow. There's a new job on.' Starr belched loudly, then hiccuped. 'Now let's get some shut-eye.'

He lurched to his feet and reeled across the room to a door at the back that gave access to his personal quarters.

'Where do I bunk down?' Luman asked. He suddenly felt exhausted. It had been a draining few days.

Starr grabbed a chair to steady himself and swung round.

'Get Vic to assign you a cot in the bunkhouse.'

Then he was gone.

SIX

SKINNING THE BEAVER

It was mid-morning of the following day when a flurry of pounding hoofs sounded through the fetid air of the bunkhouse. Only Vic Stride and the Starrbreakers' new recruit were present. The other members of the gang were out on the range, altering the brands of rustled cattle in readiness for sale. Unscrupulous Eastern buyers, aiming to take advantage of the knockdown prices, were known to hang around the fleshpots of Thermopolis.

'Must be the boss,' observed Stride who was repairing a broken stirrup. 'Let's go find out what the new job is.'

Discarding the leathers, he made for the door, followed by a curious Bob Luman, who was wondering who this mysterious leader could be. Starr had intimated that someone outside the gang was the brains behind the outfit.

If it wasn't one of these jaspers, then who in tarnation could it be?

Various possibilities filtered through his mind as he left the bunkhouse. Judging by the success of the robberies, it had to be somebody in the know, a prominent member of the local community.

The recent arrival had his back to Luman and was engaged in an earnest parley with Starr.

'Them pelts should fetch a mighty handsome return at the Flaming Gorge rendezvous,' he declared. Talk of impending raids, as always, drew a serious response from the gang leader as he addressed the slim-hipped dude whose long red hair straggled from beneath a wide-brimmed plainsman hat. 'If the pack train left Thermopolis yesterday, we've got plenty of time to reach Shoshoni Pass and give 'em a surprise they aren't expectin'. Did you say there will be four trappers ridin'. . . ?'

Starr never completed the enquiry. Noticing the arrival of the two men from the bunkhouse, he signalled for the new recruit to join them.

'Say howdy to the the brains of the outfit,' he said. Even though the lithe figure clearly had all the traits attributable to the female of the species, Luman still hadn't twigged. It was beyond his comprehension that the head honcho could be a woman.

The newcomer swung round. Her look of stunned surprise was matched by that of Bob Luman. Both were unable to contain their shock at this unexpected introduction.

Belle recovered first, quickly adjusting her posture to that of the imperious ringleader. Back stiff as a boned corset, she peered down her aquiline nose at the handsome stranger who had so recently caused mayhem in her life. The rekindling of long-dormant yearnings to be swept off her feet were suppressed as she faced the bogus escaped convict.

But Starr was no dullard and instantly picked up on the fact that these two had met before. His weathered features assumed a shadowy glare of mistrust. Acute instincts that had served him well over the years surged to the fore. His suspicions were confirmed when Luman responded by once again doffing his hat and affecting a deep bow.

'An unexpected p-pleasure,' he stammered, battling to slip back into character. His mouth opened again but nothing emerged. For once, the Bad Boy was lost for an adequate response. All he could do was smile benignly.

'It appears that the great Beavertail Bob Luman has some difficulty with a woman becoming involved in running a gang of hard-nosed desperadoes.'

Her observation was more of a question than a statement as she waited for the outlaw to reply. Starr gave the new man no time to organize his thoughts by punching out a terse interjection.

'So where did you two meet afore, then?'

'Some of the boys at the Bee Hive objected to Mr Luman's . . . erm . . . disparaging comments about Jess McCafferty's choice of hair tonic,' Belle shot back. Her sardonic reply seemed to break the tension.

Starr hawked out a raucous guffaw, hugging his side with glee. The bartender had received similar comments from others, not least the gang boss himself. But there was a welcome difference between that and having some stranger vent his spleen.

'It ain't nothing to chuckle at,' Belle rebuked her subordinate. 'This critter shot up the saloon and killed one of my best men.'

'Which one?' cut in Vic Stride, who had been drawn by the raised voices.

'Bucky Hayes,' replied the woman, eyeing the newcomer with conflicting emotions. A palpitating heart did not blend well with appreciable damage to her business and noted repute as an ice maiden.

Disdainful scepticism surged to the fore. Her reputation as the outlaw queen had to be outwardly maintained to keep Starr from suspecting her emotional bias. Still, there was no denying that the guy was a valuable asset to their enterprise.

'At least you gave Heck Ramsey plenty to think about while he's nursing that headache your fist delivered.' she said, offering a nod of approval.

Starr accorded the remark a look of puzzlement. She then went on to explain the events of the saloon debacle, purposely omitting any reference to the true reason for the gunfight. Starr chuckled blithely at the end when details of the local lawdog's chagrin were explained.

'Serves the critter right,' he gloated, slapping Luman on the back. 'Any jasper that wants to ban the totin' of hardware within the town limits deserves a good knucklin' down.'

The story of Luman's bloody encounter had only served to raise the outlaw in Starr's estimation. And Bucky Hayes was, or had been, a loudmouth and a cardsharp. He was no loss. With a casual lift of the shoulders, Starr shucked off the lethal confrontation. What happened in the confines of the Bee Hive was no concern of his. That was Belle's problem.

Now the gang leader was eager to turn the parley back to more important matters. Belle was also glad to accommodate Starr when he pressed for more information regarding the beaver-pelt mule train.

However, as to the recent gunfight, she was not as forgiving as her criminal associate. This guy might have precipitated long-dormant yearnings within her bosom, but he had been the cause of considerable damage to the saloon. And that could not remain unchallenged.

'You'll be in on this caper, Beavertail,' she said to the listening Bad Boy. 'It should be a simple job to remove a pile of skins for a guy of your experience in that field.' A casual flick of the small tail on Luman's hat received some toadyish joshing from the boys. The woman's icy smirk quickly dissolved as her mouth hardened into a thin line. 'And the damage caused to the Bee Hive will come out of your cut.'

The others laughed.

'Sure seems like a fair deal to me,' hooted Vic Stride. 'Shoot up a saloon, fella, and you gotta pay your dues.'

Luman accepted the rebuke with easy aplomb. A

slight inclination of the head conveyed his acceptance. Dark eyes locked on to those of the woman. A mutual feeling of expectancy passed between them. Something was in the air that neither quite understood.

For Drew Henry, government special agent, it was no part of his assignment to become starry-eyed over the opposition. Never in his wildest dreams could he have imagined such sentiments being occasioned by a delectable creature of Belle Sherman's ilk. But there they were, plucking at his own heartstrings.

He quickly looked away, forcing his mind back to the job in hand.

He was an agent of law enforcement, playing the role of an escaped convict, and she was an outlaw queen. There could never be any kind of future for a liaison of that nature.

Neither Leroy Starr nor his sidekick had noticed anything untoward as they got down to discussing the details of the forthcoming heist.

First light saw five of the Starrbreakers heading north for the Hole in the Wall. Leroy Starr led the way with the outlaw queen by his side. Watson and a half-breed Blackfoot known as Indian Joe had been left behind to watch over the spread.

Once the riders had crossed the Roughneck Range, Belle bid them good hunting as she turned east, back towards Kaycee.

'I'll see you boys in three days,' she said. 'By that time, the Bee Hive oughta be up and running again.'

The pointed remark was aimed at Luman. 'And I should have a buyer lined up for the furs.'

They reached Shoshoni Pass as the sun was setting over the Big Horns.

'We'll make camp in that draw,' ordered Starr, pointing to a narrow gap in the broad swath of rolling hills that would effectively hide their campfire from any prying eyes. Details like that were what had made Leroy Starr such a formidable adversary.

Luman was impressed.

'After supper, you stand first watch, Rusty. Luman here will spell you after four hours,' continued the gang leader. No voices of complaint followed the brusque directions. Starr was undisputed boss. 'According to Belle, the mule train will be coming through the pass around mid-morning tomorrow.'

Bull Montane had taken the last watch as usual. It was his job to prepare breakfast.

'Come and get it, you sons of the saddle,' the gruff voice called as a tentative sun edged a path over the serrated rim of the Big Horn Mountains.

Stretching the stiffness from aching muscles, the others huddled around the dying embers of the campfire, shovelling down a simple breakfast of refried beans and fatback. A hot mug of Arbuckles helped disperse any lingering threads of sleep and sharpen their senses for the forthcoming affray.

Time passed quickly as last-minute plans were aired, and guns checked. Then the gang took up their positions.

Luman glanced at his gold pocket watch. It showed ten in the morning. He glanced across the arena of conflict from his place of concealment. But he could see nothing. There was no sign that Shoshoni Pass was occupied by a band of hard-bitten outlaws.

The ambushers were well hidden. Starr had them spaced out at strategic intervals with military precision. He was like an army commander. Luman surmised that he must have been a ranking officer during the war. Was it any wonder that the guy had the territory sewn up as tight as a clenched fist.

The narrow ravine through which the pack train would have to come was well covered. Two bushwhackers were positioned on each side, with Starr occupying an elevated roost atop a low butte from where he could observe the approaching team of muleskinners.

Fifteen minutes ticked by. Then Luman's acute hearing picked up the agreed signal. The bird call from Starr indicated that the train had entered the far end of the pass.

Another ten minutes passed before the line of fully laden mules hove into view. The plan was to allow the train and its guardians to pass the first two bushwhackers unchallenged.

Luman was one of these, with Vic Stride his opposite number on the far side of the rock-strewn gorge. As soon as the mules had passed, both men urged their mounts from behind the covering boulders to block any retreat. At the same moment, the other two leapt out at the front.

'Don't make any sudden moves, gents,' shouted Bull Montane. The heavy-set jigger backed up his command with a Sharps Big Fifty buffalo gun. 'This is a stick-up. All we want is the furs. Hand 'em over without any ruckus and you can go free.'

Nobody moved.

'You heard the man!' snapped Rusty Laverne, waving a pair of Colt Frontiers, adding his two-bits' worth to the run-in. 'Get them hands in the air where we can see 'em!'

The train suddenly lurched to a halt. Stunned by the attack, the two leading riders instantly obeyed.

The mules, however, were less obliging. Their steady routine had been rudely interrupted. One brayed loudly, then kicked its back hoofs, catching Stride in the chest and knocking him flying. This disruption gave the other guards courage to challenge their attackers.

One drew his pistol and shot the fallen outlaw in the head. Blood poured from the fatal wound. From his elevated position, Starr jammed the Whitney & Burgess carbine into his shoulder and levered off three quick shots. The blasts echoed loudly in the confines of the ravine. But one at least found its target.

The guard threw up his arms and slid from the saddle. His horse reared up on hind legs, charging off back towards the entrance to the pass, dragging its rider by a trapped boot heel. If the poor guy hadn't been dead before, he sure was when the animal finally slowed to a snorting halt. His mashed torso was little more than a bleeding sack of broken bones.

The remaining ambushers now let fly with all the weapons at their disposal. Smoke mingling with the dust churned up by the panicking mules made accuracy difficult. Luman joined in. But he made certain that his shots went just that fraction high, to avoid hitting the remaining guards.

A scream towards the front of the train told him that another of the guards had been hit.

'Got me one of the bastards,' Luman yelled triumphantly laying claim to the glory of the fatal hit. He knew that there was no chance of his claim being challenged in the hazy gloom.

Then he heard Starr's raucous yelp above the ear-shattering clamour.

'One of 'em is gettin' away.'

Stuck in his position on the butte, the outlaw chief was unable to go in pursuit of the fleeing muleskinner. Lurid imprecations poured forth. Arms flailed impotently.

'I'll go after him,' hollered Luman, swinging his horse around and galloping off down the ravine, concealed by a thick cloud of dust.

The guard had a good head start.

Luman urged Snapper to a frenetic gallop. No need for sharp spurs. The grey knew instinctively that speed was required. Ears laid flat, the mare stretched her legs to the maximum. Fifty yards down the trail, they sped past the stationary horse and the grisly remains of its rider. Soon the distance between the fleeing guard and his pursuer measurably shortened.

Turning round in the saddle, Luman checked that the gang leader was out of sight. A plan had quickly taken shape in his mind. But what he had in mind had to be conducted in private.

Satisfied that he was not under observation, Luman tightened his knees against the horse's flank. Releasing the reins, he dragged out the Winchester from its boot. A swift up-and-down levered a round into the upper barrel.

Then. A momentary pause until the right moment before he snapped the trigger back. The zinging bullet licked the neck of the guard's horse. It was a perfect shot, a flesh wound designed to frighten the animal, make it stumble and so unseat its rider.

Although momentarily stunned, the man quickly recovered. Scrambling to his feet, he lunged for the revolver on his hip.

Luman blasted another round that kicked up sand between the guard's legs.

'Don't try it, fella,' rapped the pursuer. Jammed into his shoulder, the steady aim of the carbine was cause enough for the fallen guard to raise his hands skyward.

Having dismounted, Luman lowered his own weapon.

'There ain't much time to explain,' he said urgently, 'but I ain't no bush whacker. My name is Drew Henry and I'm a special agent with the Bureau of Detection. My assignment has been to infiltrate this gang so as to break their criminal stranglehold on the territory.'

The guard emitted a grunt of incredulity.

'How do I know you are one of them Bad Boys we've heard so much about?' he muttered. 'This could be some trick to make me surrender.'

'If'n I'd been a genuine bushwhacker, wouldn't I have just shot you down without a second thought?' The guard had no answer to that. 'And here I am giving you the chance to escape. But you gotta do something for me in return.'

The guard recognized the truth of his captor's claim. Why indeed would a genuine outlaw be parleying like this instead of gunning him down? It made sense that he must be an undercover lawman.

'OK, Mr Henry, guess I gotta believe you,' said the startled guard, who was only too pleased to have come through the ambush with his skin intact. 'What d'yuh want me to do?'

'Soon as you reach the nearest town, wire a message to my boss, Isaac Thruxton, care of the sheriff's office at Laramie.'

He drew breath, throwing a wary look to his rear. Still no sign of the other Starrbreakers. But he could not afford to delay.

A gleam flashed in Drew Henry's eye. Here was his chance to catch the leaders of the gang red-handed when they went to sell the pelts at the Flaming Gorge rendevous down on the Green River.

Following the decimation of the beaver and other fur-bearing critters, most of the annual meets had been disbanded. This was the only one still remaining. It attracted a host of n'er-do-wells hoping for some easy pickings.

The surge of excitement was, however, tempered by a sigh of regret. It was a pity about Belle Sherman. Another time, another place, and perhaps things might have been different. She sure was a feisty dame whom he could have gone for in a big way. But the outlaw queen was clearly the brains behind the outfit and had to be stopped.

'Tell Thruxton that the gang—'

He got no further as the deep throaty roar of a rifle punched through the hush. The guard threw up his arms and tumbled backwards. Another three bullets brought the guy's unexpected luck to a sudden conclusion.

Leroy Starr emerged from behind a boulder. Luckily he had been out of earshot of the conflab that had been so brutally terminated. But a measure of suspicion was etched across the scowling visage. The Whitney was held across his chest at the ready.

Taken by surprise at the sudden appearance of the gang leader, Drew quickly grasped that this was a critical moment. His features assumed a suitably twisted expression of vexation.

Then he let fly before Starr could challenge him.

'What in thunder did you go and shoot him for?' he snapped acidly. 'The guy was just about to spill the beans on another shipment of furs.'

'That palaver looked a mite too cosy for me.' The gang boss glowered, still not convinced. 'Anyway, why should he offer to give up any information to you? Don't make no sense.'

'That's cos you don't know the half of it,' Luman retorted, struggling to contain the anger that was bubbling under the surface. 'I'd just threatened to shut his lights out for good if'n he didn't cough up.'

'Ugh!' grunted Starr. 'How was I to know? You should have brought him back to the pass.' He puffed his chest out. 'I'd have soon gotten it out of him with a hot iron.'

'I don't go in for heavyweight persuasion like some.' Luman fixed an accusing gaze on the outlaw chief. 'A few menacing threats regarding his continued good health would have gotten things done a heap quicker, and more quietly too. But it's too late for that now.'

Starr shrugged. It was the nearest thing to an apology he could manage. Admission that he was at fault did not sit well with the gang leader.

Drew exhaled a sigh of relief, knowing that he had won Starr over with his quick thinking. Not wanting to antagonise the guy any further, he attempted to laugh off the shooting. Though inside he was furious. Here was a heaven-sent opportunty to smash up the gang that had gone to waste. He would now have to await another chance.

'That sure was good shooting, Leroy. You had that critter dancing a merry gig afore he went down.'

Starr liked that. Any praise of his shooting prowess went down like Ma's apple pie and cream. A huge grin spread over the weathered countenance. Then he turned away.

'Time we was outa here.'

SEVEN

UNWELCOME VISITOR

As soon as the blurred outline of the Buffalo Creek cabin sharpened into focus, Bob Luman immediately sensed that all was not right.

The sun shone bright as a button in the cloudless sky. Meadow larks swooped and cavorted in joyous abandon. And Starr had promised the men a bonus, owing to the unexpected haul of furs, which was much higher than expected. Everything should have been hunky-dory. But that itch on the back of his neck told a different story. Something was wrong.

Luman's back stiffened. The two outlaws left behind to keep watch were acting suspiciously. They were unnaturally spaced out. To the wary interloper, it was as if they were expecting trouble. The overly casual demeanour was contrived, as though it had been planned in advance to make them appear relaxed. And those hands. Resting a bit too obviously on the gun butts of their holstered pistols.

A hound dog barked as the five riders entered the corral adjoining the barn. Its constant yapping went unchecked until Starr yanked out his revolver and dispatched a slug buzzing around its ear. A frightened yelp and the mutt quickly vanished.

The narrowed eyes of Bitter Creek Watson and his Blackfoot sidekick were locked on to the tense figure of the new man. The grip on their pistol butts tightened.

Other than Luman, none of the riders had picked up on the uneasy atmosphere. They were all glad to be back, but were musing on the loss of Vic Stride. The outlaw had been with Starr from the beginning. His death at Shoshoni Pass was a personal tragedy to the gang leader as well as a setback to the gang's strength.

It was Watson who broke the silence.

'We got us a visitor in the cabin that you're gonna find mighty interestin', Leroy.'

The remark was uttered in a tightly controlled voice. Measured and flat in its delivery, it was immediately apparent to the boss that this was no ordinary arrival. That was when the crackling tension emanating from the two guardians impinged on his thoughts.

'Some'n wrong then, Bitter Creek?' he voiced curtly.

'That depends on who's tellin' the truth,' replied

Watson, quickly whipping out his revolver. The barrel was aimed at Luman's chest. 'Come on out, fella!' he called. 'And say howdy to your double.'

The door of the cabin squealed on rusty hinges.

A tall heavy-set jasper emerged. Clutched between his yellowed teeth was a bent cheroot. Like a black fang it bolstered the aura of menace oozing from his every pore. He was clad in black corduroys and a leather vest, his thumbs were hooked nonchalantly into a twin-rigged gunbelt. But it was the cold flinty gaze that propelled a shiver down Luman's spine.

He didn't need to be told who this jasper was. But Watson made the introductions anyway.

'Meet another Beavertail Bob Luman,' he spat out in a surly voice. Scratching his greasy mop of sandy hair, the outlaw muttered, 'Although it beats me who's the real one.'

For a long ten seconds nobody spoke.

Bulging eyes and gaping mouths surveyed the newcomer before flicking between the two men. The Beavertails were not alike in looks. Chalk and cheese would be an apt assessment. But as none of the Starrbreakers had set eyes on the real Bob Luman, they had no way of knowing which was the genuine article.

'There's only one Bob Luman. And that's me,' averred the newcomer bluntly.

His manner was brusque and decisive. The fervent assertion was punched out with a guttural rasp. The man in black stepped down off the veranda and planted his boots squarely in front of the Bad Boy. A curling lip sneered in disdain as he jabbed a finger at the traitor in their midst.

'This rat has to be a spy sent by the government to infiltrate this gang. There's only one way of dealin' with vermin.'

Hawking a gob of spittle at the bogus outlaw, Luman went for his gun.

But before he had a chance to draw, a gun jammed into his back. Like a wraith in the night, Indian Joe had sidled up behind the blustering newcomer.

'No shoot! Starr boss decide who is right Beavertail.' The throaty command was enough to stay the outlaw's hand.

Drew wasted no time in taking the opportunity forcefully to declare his own claim to the outlaw's reputation.

'He's lying, boss,' avouched Henry. Desperation to deny his imposture laced the impassioned denial of Luman's accusation. And there was no play-acting involved. Drew was well aware that his life was at stake. 'Ain't I already proved my worth at Shoshoni Pass? It was me that killed one of those guards remember. And that shoot-out in the Bee Hive was no set-up neither.'

It was rapidly dawning on his stunned brain that the real Bob Luman had somehow engineered an escape from the pen and come north after he'd heard about the subterfuge being played out in his name. He had rightly assumed that such a plot could only have been instigated by the law for the sole purpose of curtailing the mayhem being perpetrated by the Starrbreakers.

As none of the gang had met Luman, it was his word against Drew's. The Bad Boy risked a tentative glance to figure out which way the devious mind of the gang boss was leaning.

Starr's face was set as hard as granite as he mulled over the bizarre situation. It presented a block of stone that gave nothing away. Yet the leader was a volatile character. It was anybody's guess as to whose side he would take.

That resolution was postponed when Belle Sherman arrived.

Sharp as a tack, the outlaw queen was instantly aware of the tense atmosphere. She dragged her horse to a slithering halt.

'What's the beef, Leroy?' she snapped at her subordinate.

Starr aimed a gloved hand at the newcomer. 'This jasper has turned up claiming to be the real Bob Luman,' he replied. 'He's accusin' this fella' – a thumb jerked towards Drew Henry – 'of being a government plant sent to betray our plans. I don't know one from the other. How d'yuh figure we gonna sort it?'

For once in his life, Leroy Starr was perplexed. His bewildered features registered the confusion of his thoughts.

Belle speared the new arrival with a sceptical glower. What she saw did not sit well. The arrogant posture, the surly manner. But most of all, the sneeringly caustic appraisal of herself, which said it all. A woman's place is to make babies and keep house.

Her glance swung towards the man now under suspicion. Their eyes met. And once again, a certain unspoken accord bridged the gap. From their first meeting, Belle had sensed that the mysterious stranger was different. All the outward displays of disdainful toughness were there. But he had never quite fitted the usual outlaw mould.

Now she knew the truth. This guy was a tinstar out to break up the gang. It was hard to comprehend. She itched to come down on his side. But there was too much at stake here. Not least her and the gang's freedom. Belle Sherman did not intend to spend the best years of her life behind bars.

At that moment of indecision, the answer to her dilemma came from the unlikely mouth of Bitter Creek Watson.

'There is one way to suss out the Judas in our midst,' he muttered in a leisurely drawl.

All eyes shifted to the stocky Texan. Watson paused to light a cigar.

'Well?' exclaimed the impatient Leroy Starr. 'Spit it out then.'

Watson removed a fleck of tobacco from his upper lip before answering. 'I know for a fact that Lopez once rode with the Luman gang down Cimarron way. So he's bound to recognize the real fella. A pointed finger is all it'll take. Then,' the grinning outlaw parodied a shooting pistol, 'Bang! Bang! And the *traidor* bites the dust.'

'There's just one problem with that solution,'

commented a mocking Rusty Laverne. 'Lopez is locked up in the hoosegow at Casper.'

Starr had been listening to the interchange and liked what he had heard. He interjected with an acerbic swipe at the cocky young tearaway.

'Then we'll have to bust him out, won't we, chuck-lehead?' The sarcastic mockery was laid on thick as whipped cream. 'And in the meantime, we'll keep these two jaspers under guard in our own lock-ups.'

'You mean the two root cellars, boss?' enquired Watson.

Starr nodded. 'Shouldn't be for more than five days.' Then he laughed out loud. 'We can't have them attackin' each other. The wrong one might come out as the winner.' The sardonic smirk dis-solved into a frosty glint as he added, 'And I want to be the one to bury that snake in the grass.'

Luman uttered a feral growl, angrily contesting the suggestion that he should be thus incarcerated.

'I didn't escape from one prison to be locked up in another,' he fulminated, psyching himself up to grab for his pistol.

Indian Joe laid an iron fist over his gun hand while jabbing his pistol into the outlaw's ear.

'You do as boss say. Only way to solve problem.'

Starr laughed. 'Joe's right. You ain't got no say in the matter.'

At a signal from the gang leader both men were quickly pinioned. Starr then sidled up to the strug-gling Luman and playfully tapped his stubbly cheeks.

'And when, or if, Lopez proves you right, we'll all

have a big celebration dancing on the grave of the double-dealing trickster. You never know. It might well be you . . . Mr Beavertail.'

Insolently tugging on the telltale talisman, Starr dismissed the two captives, who were hurriedly bundled away to begin their incarceration in the less than comfortable quarters.

'Don't worry, boys,' he called after their retreating backs. 'It's only for a few days. Although for one of you, it'll be like waitin' for the hangman to arrive. And I'll be the one who'll be fittin' a tailormade noose.' The laughter was brutally coarse with no hint of levity.

Belle shivered, knowing exactly who would be sweating it out in the root cellar. Her whole being screamed out to do something, anything to thwart Starr's plan for a gruesome send-off for the man who had so unwittingly captured her heart.

The realization was sudden, unexpected and inspiring. A light had been turned on. Her previous life had been conducted in the shadows of nightmarish confrontation. And now she had emerged into the glorious light of day where the sun shone down on to an infinitely more wholesome future.

She now desperately wanted to quit the owlhooter trail for good. But would helping this enigmatic stranger to escape certain death at the hands of Leroy Starr be enough for him to back her quest to go straight? Did he have the same feelings for her? Questions and more questions hammered at her distraught brain. But what were the answers?

The outlaw queen was desperately trying to convince herself that their precarious liaison had a future. Maybe they could go away together, start up afresh someplace where the name of Belle Sherman meant nothing?

But how to go about it?

'We'll set off for Casper at first light,' she heard Starr telling the gang as the problem of saving Drew Henry filled her thoughts. 'You better head back for Kaycee, Belle,' he said. 'Send out a few of your boys to look after things here while we're away.'

Belle just sat in the saddle, unmoving, like a regal statue.

'You listenin'?' the gang leader murmured impatiently, nudging her mount. 'Look like you've seen a ghost.'

The jolt brought her back to earth with a bump. She shook off the turbulent emotions that were racking her inner being.

'Just a bit stunned by what's happened here,' she mumbled, trying to recover her composure. 'Got any leaning as to who's the magpie?'

Starr replied with a dismissive shrug. 'Won't matter none when Lopez gets here. Then we'll know for sure.'

'I'll get back to town, then. You keep them furs in the barn until this Luman business is sorted.'

'I'll have Joe get 'em ready for packin' and sendin' down to the rendezvous,' said Starr. Then another thought occurred to the gang leader. His eyes lit up. 'And we can nobble them Circle S bulls on the way.

Kill two birds with one stone, eh boys?'

'We sure are gonna be in the dough after this caper, boss,' observed Laverne. A huge grin stretched from ear to ear.

'Enough for us to retire in luxury over the winter in Brown's Park,' came back the lusty response.

The idle banter drifted over Belle's head as she swung her horse round and spurred off without another word. Starr's beady peepers followed her retreating back, a quizzical frown shadowing his angular features.

The outlaw queen was acting kinda strange, was not her usual feisty self by a long chalk. Some'n was up. Starr's frown deepened. The gal hadn't been herself since she'd set eyes on that first Luman character, who had turned up out of the blue.

But he was accorded no further chance to ponder on the issue.

'You best come over here, boss,' called out the unsettling rumble of Bitter Creek Watson. 'That latest arrival is kickin' up a right shindig.'

Starr cursed volubly. 'You tell that varmint that if'n he don't button his lip right now, there won't be any need for Lopez to point the finger. Cos I'll do it for him . . . with a bullwhip!' A quick flick of the wrist and the writhing brown serpent was snapping. A loud crack split the air.

The satisfied grunt from his sidekick was enough to reassure the gang leader that his threat had worked.

Still casting a wary eye towards the disappearing

queen of the plains, he moved away to arrange storage of the pelts.

Belle drew her mount to a halt as she crested a low rise. Shading out the lowering sun, she looked back towards the cluster of ranch buildings surrounded by an ocean of waving grass. Lines of worry that had so recently furrowed her anxious brow had now disappeared. Lips drawn tight conveyed a rugged determination.

A decision had been made.

EIGHT

BREAKOUT

Once out of sight of the Starrbreakers' ranch, she cut away to the south-east, heading for Deadman's Bluff. Casper was only a full day's ride on the far side of the Rattlesnake Hills. She dismounted behind a huddle of rocks some hundred yards back off the main trail.

There she untied her bedroll and settled down for the night.

A steely gleam in her eye matched the resolution in her soul. Relief about the determination to pursue a normal life eased away the tension in her bones. Now that her plan was being implemented, Belle felt that a heavy weight had been lifted from her shoulders.

She was under no false illusions that it would be a simple task. Leroy Starr was a vengeful desperado who would fight tooth and nail to protect the profitable enterprise they had built up together. And his retribution against those who had betrayed him would be merciless.

Disappearing with a new name and a new life was the only answer. She hoped that it might be in the company of the stranger.

A serene look graced her satin smooth features as she unpacked the saddle-bags. This was the first time the emergency rations had been called upon. Concealed from prying eyes, a fire and a hot meal would help her pass the long night in some measure of comfort.

The false dawn found Belle fully awake. Streaks of purple and orange pierced the pall of darkness as the early sun struggled above the craggy outlines of the nearby hills. After breaking camp, she hurried to the top of a low knoll and settled down to scan the trail.

She did not have long to wait.

Four hazy shadows emerged from the greyness of early morning. Belle tensed. This was her chance to put the plan for a new start into motion. After returning to the main valley trail, she checked that Starr and his boys were out of sight before swinging back towards the ranch.

Reining up in a clump of cottonwoods near the entrance gate, her piercing gaze searched for any sign of movement. Indian Joe was somewhere around. A vague recollection prodding her brain said that the Blackfoot halfbreed would likely be in the barn assembling the furs.

Then she saw him: a tall statuesque figure clad in

buckskins, a large eagle feather poking above his flat-brimmed hat. He had just emerged from the barn and was heading back to the bunkhouse. If he was anything like the others, it would be to prepare a hearty breakfast of eggs, bacon and beans.

And that meant she had a good half-hour to free the stranger and head south-west towards the Utah border, and then . . . California.

A hot flush coloured her cheeks at the thought of ridding herself of what had become a millstone around her neck.

In the beginning, dodging the law had been hypnotic and intoxicating, a potent aphrodisiac, like a drug. And highly profitable. Not to mention the satisfaction of having a bunch of hard-nosed desperadoes dancing to her tune.

But with the arrival of the mysterious stranger all that had changed overnight. It had been a sudden conversion.

There was no denying that the excitement of cocking a snook at the authorities had palled. Starr was getting far too sassy. And because she had blocked his lustful advances, there was every likelihood that in the not too distant future he would want to take over.

Belle tried to convince herself that the stranger's propitious arrival in Kaycee had merely set the ball rolling. Was she chasing shadows in expecting that an agent of the law would help her disappear, get away without any form of payback? On further reflection it seemed unlikely. But the die was cast. There was no going back now.

Luckily, Belle had stashed away a handsome poke in the national bank under a false name. There was nothing in Kaycee that she would miss.

After giving the halfbreed five minutes to settle down in the bunkhouse, she crept out from the cover offered by the desiccated trees and cat-footed across to the first root cellar.

It was no more than an eight-foot-square hole in the ground, covered by a wooden framework with a dual-hinged flap. Approaching the prison, she paused, listening out for any adverse sounds. Nothing. Only the lowing of cattle in the meadow and a faint rustling of dried leaves in the tree cover overhead. A strident grating over by the barn made her pulse quicken. But it was only a loose door that required greasing.

Holding her breath, Belle moved across to the door, praying that it had not been padlocked. A sigh of relief escaped from pursed lips when she saw the heavy outer bolt.

A shuffling inside told her that the cellar was indeed occupied.

'Can you hear me, fella?' she whispered. Her lips were pressed close to the wooden slats. The stench of rotten marrows and corn cobs made her nose wrinkle in disgust.

The shuffling stopped.

'You come to gloat then, Miss Outlaw Queen?' The reaction sounded gloomy and dejected. Drew had no doubts that Leroy Starr would figure out some method of setting Lopez free. He had become resigned to his fate once the Mexican bandit arrived and uncovered his masquerade. 'Having a laugh at the clever lawdog who's been caught with his pants down?'

'The name's Belle Sherman,' snapped the woman. 'And yeah, I know you ain't the real Bob Luman. Don't know how. Call it a woman's intuition. And I ain't the Outlaw Queen no more. I've decided to quit this game and get out while the going's good. So I'm here to help you escape as well.'

Without further ado she knocked out the bolt with the butt end of her revolver and levered up one side of the heavy door-flap. Drew screwed his eyes up against the light from the new sun which was now fully over the eastern rimrock of the Rattlesnakes. Clambering out, he eyed the woman with undisguised suspicion.

'Why are you doing this?' he queried, casting a wary peeper around the cluster of ranch buildings. Then his eyes narrowed to thin slits. 'Could be it's a trick aimed at getting me to show my hand. Then Starr can gun me down without the bother of busting Lopez out of the slammer.'

Belle arrowed him with a caustic glower.

'If'n you don't trust me, then take this.' She handed him the Colt Frontier. 'Take it!' she urged when he hesitated. 'It's fully loaded. So don't that prove I'm on the level?'

Drew was given no further chance to consider the startling offer.

'What go on here?' The gruff query came from the corner of the barn.

Indian Joe had run out of water and was heading for the well when he heard voices. A brief glance round the edge of the wooden wall told his fertile brain that skulduggery was afoot.

Why had the lady boss released their prisoner and handed over her gun?

'Why you back here, miss? And helping this man?'

Belle's mouth dropped open with shock.

Drew Henry was quicker on the uptake. His hand lifted. Snapping back the hammer, he fired. Hot lead spat from the barrel.

But Joe was no sluggard and quickly ducked behind the wall as slivers of rotten wood flew in all directions. The Indian quickly brought his own gun into action. Leaping out from cover he let fly with both barrels of the sawn-off Greener.

Belle screamed and went down, tumbling back against Drew.

In so doing, she had unwittingly saved his life. Luckily most of the shot had gone wide. But blood still poured from a myriad tiny cuts where the blast had ripped into her stomach.

Seeing his quarry bite the dust, the large Blackfoot whooped excitedly. A tethered ranch hound joined in the discordant mêlée. Then the Indian charged, emitting a blood-curdling tribal war chant, a cry intended to terrify a foe into rocklike immobility.

He threw the spent Greener aside. Then, in a single fluid motion, he snatched a tomahawk from his belt and launched the deadly weapon towards the pair of traitors. Drew instantly threw himself to one side, dragging the injured woman with him. The lethal blade buried itself in the root cellar door-flap inches from his head.

Joe growled out a demented curse and snatched the lethal hunting knife from his belt. He raised it to throw. His victims were helpless, splayed out on the ground with nowhere to go.

Still maintaining a firm grip on his revolver, the Bad Boy had three bullets left. He made each one count.

Indian Joe took them all in the stomach. Pitching forward, he came to rest in an untidy heap across the half-open cellar entrance.

Drew sucked the cooling air of early morning into his shaking body. His heart was racing faster than a desert roadrunner. As she lay atop him muted groans escaped from between the woman's tightly clenched teeth. He gently extricated himself and laid her down flat.

A brief examination was enough to make it clear that she was in great pain. Without urgent attention she would most certainly bleed to death.

It was equally clear to the exposed lawman that flight from the ranch had to be considered an urgent priority. With the wind blowing eastwards, the Starrbreakers were bound to have heard the gunshots. He had about half an hour before they returned to investigate the cause of the disturbance.

Belle groaned as a wave of agony shot through her

trembling body. Then she appeared to rally.

'Now you see . . . that I wasn't . . . playing games?' The hoarse rasp almost choked her. Another spate of coughing racked the slender frame. It precipitated a snaking line of blood that oozed from the corner of her mouth. Her eyes closed for second. Again she seemed to recover. 'I meant . . . it,' she affirmed grasping his arm. 'We can go to California . . . start over again.' A loose smile, creased with pain, played across the ashen features. 'Maybe togeth. . . ?'

The imploring query remained unanswered as Drew placed a finger on her lips.

'Hush up, Belle,' he whispered, quieting the muted ramblings. There were tears in his eyes. This woman had saved his life. 'Let's just get you fixed up first. Then we can talk.'

The struggle to assure the lawman of her fidelity and devotion were too much for the enfeebled body. She sank back in Drew's arms. Blackness, deep and unavoidable, enveloped her entire being.

Lifting the woman carefully into his arms, Drew carried her over to the ranch house. There he patched up the worst of her injuries as best he could. But a nagging sense of guilt pricked at his conscience. Unless she received the expert ministrations of a doctor within the next few days, Belle Sherman, the penitent outlaw queen, would surely die.

He hurried over to the barn and quickly backed a horse into the traces of a buggy. Belle's breathing was scratchy and weak. Almost reverently, he laid her down in the bed of the flimsy carriage.

His eyes misted over.

Ever since that first encounter at the Bee Hive in Kaycee, Drew had sensed a spark being generated between them. And it was more than just animal lust. Yet never for one minute could he have imagined that the Outlaw Queen of Wyoming would throw up everything to save his bacon like this.

He shucked off the lethargy that threatened to envelop his brain. This woman deserved every shred of ingenuity he could muster to bring her through this. And if'n it meant going against all he stood for, then so be it.

Returning to the house, he grabbed a few stores, not forgetting a rifle from among those that hung above the great stone hearth. To delay any pursuit by the Starrbreakers, he emptied a pail of coal oil on to the wooden floor. A scratched vesta flared. Soon orange tongues of flame were licking at the tinder-dry walls.

'That'll give you something to think about, Leroy.'

He laughed aloud as the crackling blaze took a firm grip on the house. But there was no hint of levity in the brittle delivery. A manic gleam of revenge was reflected by the searching tendrils of fire.

Admiring his handiwork, Drew continued his furious rant.

'And make no mistake. Once Belle has been put into the hands of a sawbones, you can bet your boots that I'll be back. Then it'll be out in the open. No sneaking around. Head to head.' Sweat burst across his brow as he backed out of the door, away from the growing conflagration. A clear eye focused on the still form in the buggy. 'No quarter asked or given. This has become personal.'

A muted squawking from the other root cellar went unanswered. The recapture of Beavertail Bob Luman would have to wait.

Then he jumped up on to the running board and leathered the horse into motion. The animal snorted in protest before succumbing to the aggressive crack of a whip flicking around its ears.

Heading east was out of the question. West towards the nearest town of Lander was the only option.

NINE

PURSUIT

The Starrbreakers were riding at a steady canter when the faint yet distinct rattle of gunfire assailed their ears. Leroy dragged his mount to a slithering halt in a cloud of dust.

'You guys hear that?' he questioned urgently.

'Sounds like a gunfight back down the trail,' observed Rusty Laverne.

'Well it sure weren't no rumble of thunder,' opined the snorting Bull.

'Gunfire at this time of day can only mean trouble,' rasped Bitter Creek Watson. 'And it's comin' from the direction of the ranch.'

'One of them Luman critters must have escaped and got hisself a gun.' Starr swung his horse around and spurred off back down the trail. 'Come on, boys!' he yelled urgently. 'Joe's on his ownsome. We can't let this varmint get away – whoever he might be.'

Pounding hoofs ate up the miles at a frantic pace as the gang headed back to Buffalo Creek. It wasn't long before they saw a black plume of smoke drifting above the rise behind which the outlaw ranch was concealed.

Starr figured the worst.

One of those damn blasted skunks had done for the Indian and then fired the ranch. His knuckles tightened on the reins as he urged his mount to a frenetic gallop. Cresting the knoll, he took in the burning ranch house below. Indian Joe was lying in a pool of blood. Starr's searching eyes panned the arena for any sign of the renegade. But the only movement was a lone buzzard circling high above the dead Indian.

Teeth were clenched tight in anger. Fury seething inside the gang leader's chest erupted in a howl of manic rage.

'Aaaaaaaaagh!'

He leathered the horse down the slope and leapt from the saddle before the animal had a chance to slither to a halt. The door-flap of one of the root cellars was wide open: the one that had so recently housed the first Luman. The obvious conclusion, even to a halfwit, was that he had been the Judas in their midst.

And now he had escaped.

A frowning glower of frustration cracked Starr's granite features as he attempted to figure out how the cellar-door bolt had been removed – from the outside. Somebody had been in cahoots with the varmint. He was given no further time to cogitate on the identity of the critter's sidekick.

The muffled sound of a raised voice broke through the heavy atmosphere. It was coming from the other root cellar. Starr hurried over and quickly released the real Bob Luman. The guy struggled out. He was twitchy and on edge, his body shaking uncontrollably.

Starr slapped him hard across the face.

'Pull yourself together,' he shouted. The gang boss was in no mood to tolerate spinelessness. 'And tell me what you know about all this.'

The sharp crack jerked the outlaw from his imminent panic attack. He cast a morose eye at the gang leader. In normal circumstances the escaped convict would have had no hesitation in gunning down the perpetrator of such an action. But he was unarmed, and realized that he had been on the point of losing control.

'Gimme a smoke,' Luman croaked out, brusquely attempting to regain some measure of bravado. 'I don't cotton to being locked up like some wild dog, and by my own kind as well.'

'You callin' me a dog?' Starr's hand dropped to his revolver.

'N-no, course not!' stuttered the blustering outlaw. 'But I didn't come all this way to join up with your bunch and then get accused of bein' a goddamned plant.'

Starr huffed some before accepting the apology. He released his threatening grip. 'We had no choice,' he rapped impatiently. 'Two jaspers claiming to be Bob Luman had to be sorted. Now we know the truth.' Then he repeated his previous question. 'So what happened? And how did that skunk get free?'

Without waiting for a response he called across to a hovering Rusty Laverne.

'You and the others organize some buckets to douse this blaze. The house can't be saved but we don't want it spreading to the other buildings.'

Then he turned back to face Luman, anger at being duped once again getting the better of him.

'Come on then, Mr Beavertail. Spill!'

'All I know is that I was woken up in that stinkin' rat hole.' Luman flicked a wrinkled snout towards his recent malodorous billet. 'By a passel of gunfire. The Indian called out a challenge to someone. Then there was more shootin'.'

'And who was the mysterious visitor? Did he call out a name?' Once again Starr's short fuse was getting the better of him. 'Anythin' that could identify the skunk.'

'Had to be a woman!' Luman's reply was precise, a definite avowal. The gang boss stiffened. Luman smiled, knowing he now had the upper hand. 'Ever heard a guy referred to as . . . *Miss*?'

Starr's weathered contours assumed a purple flush of anger. He slammed a balled fist into the palm of his hand.

'Belle!' he screamed out loud. 'I'll skin her darned hide for this.' Now it all fell into place. The strange manner, withdrawn and distant. The furtive looks she thought had gone unnoticed. And all since that snake had arrived on the scene.

'Any notion which way they went?' he demanded furiously.

Luman responded with an impotent shrug.

Starr's agile brain was racing like a thoroughbred stallion. The entire future of the Starrbreakers depended on running these critters to ground. Belle was capable of leading a posse through Hole in the Wall blindfolded. If that happened Buffalo Creek would vanish overnight as a refuge for all manner of owlhoots.

But which route had they taken out of the valley?

Starr cast his baleful gaze towards his men as they tossed buckets of water at the rampaging inferno. A mournful sigh of exasperation hissed from between clenched teeth. They had as much chance of putting it out as of a snowball surviving in Hell.

Bitter Creek Watson had just emerged from the barn. He signalled across for Starr to join him. Luman followed along behind.

'The buggy ain't here.' Watson slung a thumb towards the stall where it was normally kept. 'That blackleg must have taken it.'

Starr's eyes lit up.

'That's right, Bitter Creek,' murmured the suddenly rejuvenated gang leader. 'You've hit the nail on the head. But why take a slow buggy rather than horses?' He paused, a grim frown clouding his face.

It was Luman who provided the answer.

'Unless one of them was hurt bad.'

Starr slapped the new recruit warmly on the back.

'This guy ain't just a pretty face.' The boss was grinning like the cat that got the cream. 'He's got brains under that Beavertail hat.'

Watson laughed.

'So all we gotta do now is follow the tracks,' added the new man, eminently pleased that he had now been accepted into the ranks of the much revered Starrbreakers.

'They can't get up any speed ridin' one of them clumsy traps,' observed Watson catching the boss's animated mood. 'Set off now and we could catch 'em afore sundown.'

'Then what we awaitin' on?' snapped Starr. He called across to the firefighters. 'Forget that, boys. We're off huntin', and not for rabbits.'

The tracks of the buggy were easy to follow. Twin ruts cutting deep into the soft sand could be seen way ahead. Only when the wagon crossed rocky stretches did the clear trail briefly disappear. The steady westward direction of the buggy was a dead giveaway to the pursuing outlaws. They quickly picked it up again.

Knowing that he was blazing a trail that a blind man could follow, Drew had at first made an effort to brush it out. But with Belle badly wounded and unable to help, such a precaution was much too time-consuming. Starr would catch up before they had the chance to reach the foothills of the Big Horns, where their trail would become far more dificut to follow.

Every few minutes, Drew cast a worried eye to his rear. Each time he expected to see the telltale sign of a rising dustcloud.

Belle was showing signs of getting worse. Her skin was waxy and pale as a ghost, her breathing shallow and irregular. Frequent halts were necessary to change the dressings. She had lost a lot of blood. Discolouration around the ragged wounds indicated that infection would set in without proper attention. And even to a layman, it was clear that severe internal injuries were the main problem.

Lander was on the far side of the range of bluffs that were a constant and unyielding barrier on this side of the hidden valley. What had been a welcome refuge for generations of outlaws had become a hostile barrier.

Keeping parallel with the unending barricade of red sandstone, Drew prayed earnestly to the God he had forsaken to provide him with a breach in the solid ramparts.

A series of pained groans made him bring the buggy to another juddering halt.

'You take it easy, Belle,' he whispered to the woman. Drew dampened his bandanna and dabbed her forehead, wiping away the trickle of blood from her mouth. 'We'll soon have you in the care of a sawbones.'

Belle appeared to rally. Her eyes assumed a steely glint. An unsteady hand pointed to a rift in the rock wall.

'Antelope Canyon . . . lies behind them boulders

. . . can't see it from here.' Her breathing became laboured, rasping in her throat. 'Only way through . . . from this end . . . of valley.'

The taxing effort to convey this vital information had taken its toll. Belle sank back, shoulders slumped, head drooping. Drew covered her shattered body, then looked up towards the heavens.

'Thank you, Lord,' he murmured, crossing himself.

Gently easing the team towards the rocky fissure, he guided the buggy between loose scree that covered this little-used trail. For ten minutes all went well. Then it happened. The good Lord had decided that things were going a little too smoothly.

A sharp crack rent the air. The buggy lurched. Its back wheel had slid into a deep rut and the axle was broken.

Drew cursed aloud and shook a clenched fist.

'Mighta known I'd have to work for your darned help,' he grumbled at the the invisible Creator. 'Well, we ain't scuppered yet. I'll make it outa here. With or without your support.'

But without the buggy, he was now obliged to walk out of this god-forsaken wilderness on foot and carying a badly injured woman.

Gently he levered Belle out of the useless contraption and lifted her on to his back. Her slim form was no burden as he set off up the canyon. A half-hour later his arms were aching. Even a sack of feathers makes its weight felt eventually. Girding his loins, he pressed on, gritting his teeth against the burning agony that seared his tired muscles.

As he rounded a bend in the vertical wall of Antelope Canyon, he came across a rock fall that had effectively blocked the narrow gap.

A sigh of exasperation escaped from between gritted teeth.

However, a closer inspection indicated that it was just possible, with care, to negotiate the great heap of shattered rock on foot. Drew smiled to himself. Starr was in for a shock when he and his boys arrived and were forced to abandon their horses. Yet even cast afoot, the outlaws would be able to move significantly faster than a man encumbered by an injured woman.

The moment of truth had arrived.

A single rifleman could hold off an army from up there. He filled the two canteens from a spring trickling out of a crack at the base of the fall. The climb above the flat sandy floor of the canyon was crippling. On more than one occasion he slipped back down the loose debris. Rivers of sweat poured out of him as he gamely plodded up through the tumbled mass of boulders.

Eventually he made it to a level section. There he was able to lay Belle down in the welcome shade of an overhang. Out in the open, however, Drew enjoyed no such relief. The searing heat of a brutally oppressive sun was made all the more intense within the confines of the canyon walls.

Jacking a round into the breech of his Winchester, the Bad Boy prepared to prove that his nickname was no idle boast. He hoped that the imminent confrontation would not be protracted. For Belle's sake more than his own.

His wish came sooner than expected.

A pounding of hoofs reverberated loudly within a billowing mist of yellow dust. The strident complaints of men frustrated in their mission of revenge drifted up from below. Drew was unable to pick up the actual words of the discourse, but it was clear that an angry tirade was being directed his way.

'Come and get me, you bastards,' he yelled, dispatching a couple of shells at the milling throng. 'And receive a tongue-lashing from President Winchester.'

None found its mark. But the screaming ricochets had the effect of scattering the outlaws, who dived for cover.

'You can't escape, tinstar,' the gang leader hollered back, replying with a flurry of his own lead bullets. 'Why not surrender while you can still walk outa here? I'll go easy on yuh both. Nobody can say that Leroy Starr ain't a fair man. What d'yuh say?'

Drew turned to Belle.

'You heard him, Belle. You need attention from a doctor. And you ain't getting that up here.'

Belle sucked in a couple of sharp breaths before punching out an acid response to the suggestion.

'I'd trust . . . a sidewinder . . . more'n that . . . skunk.' The virulent snarl caught in her throat. She coughed, hawking up a thick lump of congealed blood. 'And there's . . . that critter you . . . impersonated. He ain't gonna . . . let you walk . . . away.'

Then she seemed to rally. 'You get outa here. My time on this earth is over.'

'Don't say that,' protested the distraught lawman. 'I'll get you out of here somehow.'

Belle shook her head. 'I'm goin'. I know it. So listen up.' Summoning a last effort, she levered herself up on to one elbow. 'Leroy intends stealing the Circle K bulls on his way to the rendezvous.' She tugged at Drew's sleeve. 'You gotta stop him.' Drew just stared at the drawn features, tears welling in his eyes. 'Promise me!'

He gave a gentle nod, his head bowed in sorrow. When he looked up, the Outlaw Queen was dead. Desperately he clutched her to his chest. Only the renewed firing from below dragged him back to the reality of his dire situation.

With only a revolver and the shells left in his rifle, the future looked bleak. Eventually, Starr's overwhelming firepower would win the day. But until then, Drew had the advantage of height and the control of the only way out of Antelope Canyon.

For the next hour, an irregular pattern of shooting echoed off the bare rock walls. Starr's men had begun to creep closer, aiming random shots from the ample cover afforded. Drew replied with the occasional shot to deter any sudden assault on his position. But his stock of ammunition was limited. What would happen when it ran out?

He had decided to save a round for himself rather than give Starr the satisfaction of finishing him off.

Time passed in a haze of dreamy reflection. Drew

Henry was resigned to his fate. His ammunition was virtually exhausted. He lay down beside the still warm body of Belle Sherman.

And that was when he saw it.

TEN

CLIMB LIKE A DEER

Angling a jaundiced gaze to one side, he noticed a gully slanting diagonally across the face of the sheer canyon wall. Unseen until this moment, it had come to prominence with the lengthening shadows of the late-afternoon sun. Some ancient splitting of the rock had cause a narrow shelf to jut out from the main cliff. Could it offer a means of escape?

Musing on this possibility, the notion was confirmed by a deer scampering up the stony track, thus indicating how the canyon had acquired its name. Carefully following the progress of the agile creature, Drew saw it disappear over the upper rim, its dark profile etched against the azure backdrop.

The time to shift his ass was at hand. The hand of God? Perhaps.

Drew covered Belle's body with a scattering of stones to protect her from scavenging predators. The varmints down below ranked alongside coyotes, so a layer of sand was added. Only an astute observer would notice where the ground had been disturbed. And Starr would likely assume that the pair of fugitives had continued up over the rockfall.

He knelt beside the shallow mound looking up to the wide blue yonder for a sign. There was none.

'Cain't figure you out, mister,' he burbled aloud. His gaze lowered to the makeshift grave. 'Give with one hand. Then take with the other.' This time, he peered towards the narrow crack. Already it was disappearing as lengthening shadows steadily ate up the vivid relief. 'Maybe I just don't cotton to your way of thinking.'

The lawman's pensive deliberations were interrupted by a sharp crack. A slug gouged a furrow in the rock inches from his head, buzzing off with a harsh whine. Drew ducked out of sight. He shook his head in exasperation.

'There you go again,' he railed. 'Making life difficult.'

He only had three shells left.

Peeping round the edge of a covering boulder, he witnessed Starr crossing to the far side of the trail below. There was no time for a concentrated aim. But Drew's prowess with a rifle was legendary amongst the Bad Boys. A rapid-fire single round lifted the outlaw boss's hat high into the air.

A yelp of shock easily carried up to his strategic

position as the holed Stetson floated gently back down to earth. It settled on a protruding organ-pipe cactus and would have been a comical sight had not the seriousness of his situation occupied Drew's thoughts. Nonetheless, witnessing Starr diving for cover behind a boulder elicited a yip of elation.

'Come any closer and it'll be your head next time,' he trilled merrily.

A flurry of angry gunfire drove him back down into cover. But the finely tuned accuracy of Drew's shot was sufficiently effective to keep Starr from making any foolhardy moves to rush his position.

All he needed was another half-hour for the light to fade. Enough to follow the deer track safely, but forcing the Starrbreakers to make camp for the night. No way would the gang risk a frontal assault in the dark.

When he judged that the time was right, he fired the last two bullets, to remind the critters that he was still around, and willing to put up a fight. Then, keeping out of sight, Drew discarded the Winchester and edged across to the far side of the canyon where the canting gully disappeared beneath the fall of rock.

Viewed from directly below, the ascent of the narrow cutting was much steeper than he had expected. Yet the fleet-footed antelope had scurried up the precipitous incline with barely a faltering step. Drew Henry was no nimble deer. But it was his only chance to outwit the Starrbreakers.

Fingers gripping hold of the angular projections

jutting out of the cliff face, he began the long haul up the perilous slope. Luckily, his progress was hidden from those below by a lip of rock that acted as a safety barrier.

That was when the fickle nature of the weather patterns within mountain terrain decided to make life even more hazardous. Within the space of ten minutes the clear blue sky had been swallowed up by a dense mantle of grey cloud. Darkening by the second, it wasn't more than a couple of heartbeats before the first heavy droplets of rain began hammering at his exposed back.

Urged on by a screaming wind akin to the howling lament of a thousand banshees, the rain sheeted down, turning the narrow trail into a mud slick. A gushing torrent was soon pouring down on to the climber's exposed head.

His hat disappeared in the thundering downpour. Totally saturated, his body was pummelled into submission. Small stones, sharp and angular, cut his unprotected skin, rivulets of blood mingling with the rainwater. Any sort of progress under such horrendous conditions, either up or down, was impossible.

He was stuck fast like a drowned rat, his body jammed into a crack. At least it offered some protection from the fierce elements that Mother Nature was throwing at him. His only consolation was that the gang would also have been subjected to the same assault.

All he could do was weather out the storm.

Above his precarious roost, a sharp crack assailed

his battered senses. A tree had snapped under the incessant violence of the storm. The grating wrench of roots being torn from their weak footings was followed by a growling rumble. It grew to a roar as the severed trunk came trundling down the gully. Crashing against the fractured sides, it was a miracle that Drew esaped unscathed. Leaves and sharp twigs whipped across his wet cheeks, drawing more blood. Then the danger was past, smashed to a pulp far below on the rockfall.

Luckily, the furious onslaught passed over rapidly.

A rather bemused sun emerged from hiding. However, it soon regained any lost temerity. Steam rose in clouds from the climber's saturated clothes. He waited a half-hour, gathering his strength until it felt safe to continue.

The wind still howled, plucking at his clothes. All he could see was the rock in front as he groped for holds. Once again he began to climb, tentatively at first, testing each rock hold. Muscles jarred, screaming in protest when he kept slipping back down the loose muddy scree. Straining and pulling, he focused all his energies into the next drag upwards.

On one occasion the protective lip of the gully disappeared. Only a narrow shelf, no more than a foot wide, separated the rock wall from oblivion. So intent was Drew on his climb that he almost fell. A blind grab saved his life. Hanging over the yawning chasm, his arm grasping on to a jutting projection, his heart leapt as loose stone tumbled into the black abyss.

Light had almost disppeared. Dusk was settling

over the bleak landscape.

How much longer to the top? He had no way of knowing. All he could do was keep going. One foot after the other. Ever upwards. Drew now realized that trying to emulate the antics of a spritely deer had been extreme folly. But there was no way back. He rested his back against the rock face, drawing in lungfuls of air. Sweat dribbled down his face, stinging bloodshot eyes.

After the short breather, he turned to continue. Time passed in a haze of pain. Only sheer grit and determination kept the Bad Boy going.

Then suddenly, there was a break in the pattern of climbing. No more ascent. A vast panorama opened up before his bleary gaze. He had made it to the top. The wind had settled to a steady breeze, warm and comforting to his exhausted frame. Lying prostrate, flat on his back, Drew Henry closed his eyes. And slept.

Light was turning the grey dawn to a scintillating ribbon above the eastern rim of the Big Horns when Drew was suddenly jerked awake.

A raucous cawing jabbed his lethargic brain cells. Forcing his eyes open, the blurred scan revealed a skulking coyote. Slavering jaws were pulling at his boots. A blood-curdling growl accompanied the manic assault.

'Off! Off! Yuh darned scavenger!' The startled outcry emerged as a croaking rasp. He quickly sat up, lashing out at the cringing animal. The torn boot caught the beast and sent it scurrying out of range.

'There ain't gonna be no free breakfast for you, buddy,' he shouted.

A hand grabbed for the holstered pistol. Hauling back the hammer, he aimed the gun.

Then he remembered. The sound of any shot would easily carry back to the gang, who were doubtless still waiting in the canyon below. Instead, he picked up a rock and hurled it at the retreating coyote. It ran off uttering a manic howl of indignation.

But there might be others in the vicinity. They frequently hunted in packs. He scrambled to his feet and headed away from the yawning chasm of Antelope Canyon, pointing his feet west, away from the rising sun.

Drew Henry was right.

The Starrbreakers had also been forced to seek shelter from the raging storm, although for them it had been much less of a nerve-racking experience. No danger for them of being effortlessly brushed off a perilous roost like a fly off a wall. Plenty of cover was available amidst the fallen rocks in the bottom of the canyon. It had merely been a question of passing an uncomfortable night.

They emerged next morning no worse for the experience.

Mid-morning found Leroy restive and impatient. There had been no further reply to the intermittent gunfire that his men had kept up since dawn.

'You figure they went over the rockfall during the

night, Leroy?'

Bob Luman had run across from the far side of the gorge to join the boss. The skittering dash had brought no answering response from the heights above.

Starr frowned. His thoughts were moving along a similar track.

'Stick your hat on a rifle and poke it above the rock,' he said, fingering the ragged hole in his own headwear. 'It sure got a response yesterday.'

Luman did as ordered.

Nothing. Silence reigned.

Both men squinted, trying to pick up any sign of movement in the rocks, but with no success. Gingerly they stood up, bodies tense and ready to drop down again. But still there was no reaction.

'OK, boys!' Starr called across to the others. 'Make your way up through the rocks. But keep your eyes peeled. That varmint could be playin' possum.'

Guns drawn, the four outlaws carefully picked their way up through the chaotic boulder field until they reached the shelf where Henry and the girl had made their stand. An array of discarded cartridge shells told its own tale. The pair of fugitives had gone. And the only way was up.

'Sooner them than me,' voiced a sceptical Rusty Laverne. 'And in that storm, my bet is they came to a sticky end.'

The others nodded in agreement. Nobody could have survived such a horrendous buffeting in the dark. Higher up the rockfall, yawning chasms appeared amongst the fallen rocks. The slightest slip of a boot would mean certain death. Even in daylight, the climb was a less than inviting prospect.

The angle of the early sun meant that none of them had noticed the narrow deer track up which Drew had escaped.

'Better make sure,' ordered Starr moving catlike through the mound of fallen boulders.

Ten minutes later a call from over to the right brought the tentative advance to a halt.

'Over here, boss,' hollered the excited voice of Bitter Creek Watson. 'I've found some'n.'

When the outlaws had assembled under the soaring overhang of the canyon wall, Watson produced a battered Stetson. It had been snatched from Drew's head during the storm. It was ample evidence for Leroy Starr to conclude that their quarry had indeed failed to escape.

He peered into the yawning gulf.

'Good riddance to scabby traitors,' snarled Starr. He hawked a lump of phlegm into the black abyss. 'Now we don't have to bother about them rotten skunks givin' away our hideout to the law.' With a sneering grunt, he threw the hat down the hole. 'Come on, boys,' he called, in a more upbeat tone of voice. 'We got pelts to sell, and bulls to rustle.'

'Then let's kick some dust.' Beavertail Luman led the way back down to ground level. Reinvigorated, he was eager to make his presence felt as one of the infamous Wyoming Starrbreakers.

ELEVEN

ANGEL OF MERCY

Meanwhile, Drew Henry had begun his arduous trek back to civilization.

It was a daunting prospect. On his reckoning, the nearest settlement was Lander. But that was a long fifty miles due west. In all directions, as far as the eye could see, soaring mountains cloaked in dense thickets of pine jostled for position. The Big Horns were home to a breed of wild sheep that could be quite as aggressive as the notorious grizzly when surprised.

Drew would need to keep his wits to avoid unwelcome encounters with either brute beast. Wary eyes flicked about his immediate environment. A nervous twitch warned of the need to maintain a constant vigil in the harsh wilderness into which he had been pitched.

Being cast adrift without a horse did not bode well for the future either. Western riding-boots were not designed for lengthy footslogging.

The notion precipitated a shiver of dismay down his spine. All Drew had left, following the mind-numbing climb out of the abyss, were the clothes on his back. His throat felt drier than the desert wind. He shook the water bottle slung over his shoulder. It felt empty even though he had filled it before climbing.

A grim frown replaced the optimistic look of determination and relief at having survived the climb. One look was enough. It had been holed. At least he still had the revolver commandeered from Indian Joe. It was lucky that the holster was of military design with a flap that had shielded the gun during the storm.

He quickly checked to ensure its reliability. Protection against feral predators together with the chance for a hot meal helped to raise his flagging spirits. But he needed water, and fast.

He set off across the flat-topped mesa at a brisk pace. But his headway soon faltered. Negotiating the extensive plateau proved to be a gruelling test of both mind and body. Steep fissures cut down into the flat-topped mesa. Each one had to be carefully negotiated to reach the far side.

By late afternoon exhaustion forced an early halt. And still he had not come across a stream. Sucking on a pebble to stimulate the saliva flow, he eventually settled down over the stringy rabbit he had managed to shoot. Even bringing that down had wasted half his meagre stock of bullets.

Sometime during the night he was awoken by a manic howl. It was close by. The small fire was barely more than a flicker of dying embers. But there was enough light to reveal a pair of blood-red eyes staring at him from the far side of the clearing.

Another rasping growl cut through the black shadows cast by the dim light. Drew's blood froze in his veins.

A wolf! But was it alone or part of a pack? The proposed victim was given no time to consider the matter as the lethal predator moved closer. Crouching low to the ground, it was getting ready to pounce. Drew nervously reached out for his revolver.

But in the dark, it eluded his questing fingers. Panic gripped his innards. The sweat of fear leant a frantic urgency to his scrabbling hands.

Sensing the man's trepidation, that he was at its mercy, the wolf uttered a chilling howl . . . and lunged forward. Drew's terrified eyes fastened on to the charging beast, his mouth hanging open.

Then he found it.

The gun rose, the hammer was racked to full cock before discharging its lethal cargo. Orange tongues of flame spat from the barrel, illuminating the slavering jaws. Three shots rang out until the hammer clicked on to an empty chamber. Only one had found its target.

But that was enough to stymie the beast's hunger-driven attack.

It flopped down beside the prone man. The intended victim quickly scuttled away out of reach, just in case. But there was no need. The creature was finished. Nerve endings twitched involuntarily, a macabre death rattle rumbling in its throat.

Drew rolled on to his back and sucked in the cool night air. It felt like pure nectar. He lay still for what seemed like an hour. In fact, it was barely more than five minutes.

Then, fatigue, total and enveloping, claimed his addled brain.

The cold light of dawn brought home the desperate nature of his situation. No bullets were left, and only the night dew coating the sparse grass provided moisture to slake his raging thirst. Gritty eyes fastening on to the dead carcass of the wolf brought a shiver to the lawman's aching muscles.

Coaxing the smouldering embers of the fire back into life, he took out his knife and hacked a lump of flesh off the flank of the animal. It provided some sustenance to keep him going, however obnoxious it tasted.

After satisfying the hunger pangs gnawing at his guts, Drew set off once again.

It took the rest of the day to pick a tortuous route down through the jumbled rock-strewn chaos on to the open plain below. For two days he staggered west, following a course set by the setting sun. Halfway through the third day, he collapsed in a heap. Unable to take another step forward, he sank to his knees, then keeled over.

The excited squawking from a dozen vultures circling above went unheeded. Drew Henry had resigned himself to shaking hands with the Grim Reaper.

An agitated flurry of barking brought a frown to the girl's concentrated expression. Along with other hands from the Circle K, Gabby Kendrick was in the process of rounding up strays to be branded ready for the trail to market in Cheyenne. Gabby pulled her mount to a halt. A puzzled frown furrowed her brow.

What was bothering the dog? Normally a calm, stoic hound, Duke was not usually given to the frantic outbursts now assaulting the girl's ears.

The cattle were getting restive.

'Duke! Duke!' she hollered angrily. 'Over here. Now!' But the dog ignored the summons. 'What in tarnation has gotten into that darned mutt?' Her bellicose utterance was directed at Razor Sharp. 'He's over in that clump of trees. Go see what's causing all the ruckus.'

Sharp wheeled his saddle pony around and galloped off towards the source of the rowdy tumult. He disappeared into the cluster of cottonwoods.

Almost immediately the din subsided to a low keening. Gabby reined in her mustang and waited. Impatience tinged with foreboding registered across the dust-smeared profile. Something was wrong. She could feel it in her bones.

'Over here, boss,' came back the urgent call from among the trees.

Gabby instantly picked up on the alarm punctuating the cry as she leathered her cayuse through the clumps of thornbush that littered the grazing land. Prickly needles that clutched at her as she charged forward were brushed aside by the heavy batwing chaps that all ranch hands wore.

The mustang was not so lucky. Streaks of blood dripped down its flanks as the anxious rider dug in the spurs. But cow ponies are tough and well used to the harsh treatment often meted out during a round-up. Gabby's sole thought rested on what she would discover in the copse.

Duke was sniffing at the heels of a man laid out on the ground. A rough tongue licked at the scuffed leather soles. The guy looked in a bad way. Sharp was dribbling water between cracked lips. He looked up as Gabby crashed through the bushes. Dragging her mount to a juddering halt, she leapt from the saddle and hurried across.

'It's that guy who saved the bulls from being stolen by them rustlers,' exclaimed a startled Ben Sharp. 'What in thunder is the jasper doin' out in this barren wasteland?'

There would be no answer to that question until the guy regained consciousness. Gabby's heart lurched. Her pulse beat a rapid tattoo inside her chest. The notion of seeing the handsome paladin again had been discarded. Once they had parted company near Casper, ranch work had taken over her thoughts.

'Go tell Rooster to bring the chuck wagon over here so's we can get him back to the ranch.'

Ben Sharp didn't need a second bidding.

Gabby dribbled some more water into the swollen mouth.

'Not too much, Drew,' came a whispered sigh. Now that she had been left alone with the stranger, her tone assumed a note of concerned affection. She dabbed a wet bandanna across his blistered face. 'Can't have you going sick on me now.'

The man's eyes flickered momentarily as the life-giving liquid penetrated his desiccated body. A groan escaped from between parched lips. He struggled to rise, but the effort was too much. And once again he lapsed into a state of insensiblity.

Not until after sundown did Drew Henry struggle back into the land of the living. Pale eyes flickered open. A blurred image slowly tightened into focus. He forced a weak smile.

'Am I in heaven?' he slurred, his voice cracked and tremulous.

'No, just the ranch house of the Circle K,' purred a voice with the consistency of thick treacle.

'Has to be Heaven,' repeated the patient forcing a grin across his ravaged features. 'Otherwise I wouldn't be in the presence of such a pretty guardian angel.'

Gabby blushed. But the endearment made her heart skip a beat. Nonetheless, she brushed aside any amatory thoughts to concentrate on spooning the thick beef stew into the patient's mouth. But she couldn't erase the principal question that had been on all their lips.

What was this guy doing on foot wandering about in the badlands?

Another speaker who had just entered the room put the same query into words. 'You had us worried for a while, fella,' said Frank Kendrick. 'Figured you was a goner for sure. If old Duke hadn't nosed you out, you sure would have been knockin' on them pearly gates.' A quizzical frown creased the rancher's broad forehead. 'What in tarnation were you doin' out there?'

'It's a long story,' murmured Drew. He struggled to sit up. 'There's stuff needs doing that can't wait.' Again he tried getting out of the bed. But the effort drove a stab of pain through his bandaged head.

'Best you rest up for a spell,' urged the ministering angel, restraining him with gentle hands. 'No sense going off half-cocked.' The concerned fussing was replaced by a severe frown. 'Now you durned well eat this broth that I made special. It'll help build up your strength.'

'Yes, ma'am.' Settling back on to the comfortable pillows, he affected a mock salute as the tasty concoction slid down.

Once he had finished, Gabby urged him to get some sleep.

But Drew had other things on his mind, which urgently needed addressing.

Shrugging off another wince of pain he carried on, undeterred by the gentle coaxing of Gabby Kendrick to take it easy.

'We ain't got time for that now,' he protested

firmly. 'Just so's you know the truth, I'm a special agent sent by the Bureau of Advanced Detection. My job is to hunt down and arrest the gang that's been causing all this mayhem in the territory.'

Gabby's green eyes lifted in surprise.

'I figured you weren't no ordinary cowpoke, the way you handled them rustlers,' said Frank nodding his head. 'But what does a day or two matter?'

'I got it from the horse's mouth that them critters are planning to complete what they started and failed to do before.' The lawman's keen stare willed the pair of ranchers to heed his warning.

'You don't mean. . . ?'

'They're after lifting them bulls, then driving them south to sell at the rendezvous at Flaming Gorge, along with a heap of stolen beaver hides,' interrupted a rejuvenated Drew Henry. That stew had sure hit the mark. 'And it could be any day now. We gotta stop them.'

But four days of desperate wandering in the badlands had taken their toll. He sank back on to the bed, sweating from the exertion.

Gabby threw a worried look towards her brother.

'What we gonna do, Frank?'

'They won't come in the dark,' replied her brother seriously.

'How'd yuh figure that?' Gabby shot back waspishly. 'It didn't stop the varmints last time. And without Drew here to help us out, they would have succeeded.'

'That was in territory they knew,' emphasized

Frank calmly. He was well used to his sister's feisty manner and knew how to handle it. 'Our spread will be unknown to them. Starr and his bunch can only pull a successful heist during the hours of daylight.' He paused to draw breath, angling a raised eye towards the debilitated lawman.

'Your brother is right, Gabby,' Drew concurred. 'Our job now is to set a trap to bag the sneaky rats. And that'll need some careful thought.'

'You leave that to us,' said Frank standing up, 'we'll go talk it over with the boys while you get some much needed shuteye.'

He motioned for Gabby to follow him. But the girl was little inclined to abandon her newly acquired job of nurse. Frank sensed something other than professional concern in the girl's behaviour. The way she looked wistfully at the patient with those big green eyes. And the new hairstyle tied up with a red silk ribbon was a dead giveaway.

He allowed himself a fraternal smile of approval. Nothing would please him more than for his kid sister to settle down, and wear a dress for a change.

But the patient needed rest if he were to be of any help in the coming showdown.

'Gabby!'

The blunt summons was not to be ignored. Reluctantly, the girl tore herself away. A gentle snore informed the pair that their surprise guest had already succumbed to the medicinal properties of Morpheus.

TWELVE

MAKING PLANS

'How yuh feelin' this mornin', then?' enquired a rather tense Frank Kendrick from the far side of the breakfast table.

The lean-limbed rancher knew that today could well be a make or break time for them all. But at least they would have the benefit of that all-important element of surprise on their side.

It was still dark outside, although a hint of the false dawn was already lightening the sky. Somewhere out on the rimrock a lone coyote heralded the new day with its wailing lament. The sombre gathering could only hope and pray that their own fortunes would have a more uplifting finale.

Between mouthfuls of a mammoth home-cured bacon sandwich, Drew Henry muttered a garbled response. 'I feel fitter than a stag in the rutting season.' A hand flew to his mouth when he realized that the lady of the ranch was hovering by his elbow. 'My apologies, Gabby. Didn't know you was around.'

The girl laughed off the ribald comment. 'Being the only woman on a ranch means I get to hear a sight more'n that every day. You get used to it.'

'And she can give as much back when she's a mind,' came the chuckled reply from her brother.

'Must be that stew you served up last night,' said Drew, anxious that the girl didn't look on him as just another loose-mouthed roustabout. 'Not to mention the much-appreciated care and attention I received.'

Frank took the hint and changed the subject.

'We raise the finest beef west of the Great Divide on the Circle K,' he stressed proudly. 'Ain't that so, Gabby?'

'Sure is. And those bulls are gonna make the quality of our stock famous from Texas to the Canadian border.'

Talk of the prize bulls brought them back to the matter in hand.

'How do you want to play this, then?' Drew asked, fixing the rancher with a penetrating regard. 'You fellas know the lie of the land better than I do. But I reckon it would be best to lure them into a tight corner. Some place where they can be corralled.'

Kendrick considered the matter with a tight-knit expression.

'I've got three of the boys up on the heights overlooking the ranch buildings.' He selected a cigar from the humidor and offered one to their guest. Both men lit up before the discussion continued.

'That way we'll have a least a half-hour's warning of any approaching riders.'

'Where have you got the bulls corralled?'

'A mile east of here there's a shallow box canyon where we usually keep our remuda. The bulls have been penned up in there. Any riders passing the entrance can easily spot them. And it's out of sight of the ranch.'

Gabby cut in with her own contribution. The girl had no intention of being left out in the cold when it came to thwarting the intended stock theft. 'We figured that the gang would be deterred from making a frontal assault on well-guarded ranch buildings.'

Drew responded with a sagacious nod of approval.

'Sounds good to me,' he averred, sipping the hot coffee.

'It'll be like shootin' fish in a barrel,' chortled a grizzled old jasper who had just sidled in from the kitchen.

'Soon as the boys see anything suspicious, they'll warn us with a special owl hoot.' Kendrick laughed, jabbing a thumb at the newcomer. 'Old Rooster Langley here is our cook. He learned it during the War. Reckons it saved his hide after they were routed at Bull Run and it was every man for himself.'

'If'n yuh do it right,' butted in the old dude while dishing up some fresh baked biscuits, 'nobody can tell the difference from the real thing. He laid down the blackened tray and pursed his thick lips. The haunting call echoed mournfully around the small room.

Smiles all round were followed by a burst of appreciative applause as the performance ended.

'And with the wind in our favour, you'll hear it easy.' The old cook looked at the sceptical faces ranged around the table. Adjusting a battered union cavalry hat he added, 'Don't you guys even consider leavin' ol' Rooster outa this caper.' His gruff reproof brooked no dissension. He was going and that was an end of the matter. 'I've been a-cleanin' up my old Springfield just in case them varmints decided on another crack at the bulls.'

Frank shrugged his broad shoulders.

'There ain't no denyin' that we can sure use an extra gun.'

'That's settled then.' The ageing veteran appeared satisfied as he fussed about clearing up the empty plates. 'I'll leave the washin' up 'til we get back.'

An owl hoot sounded outside.

It was the signal for the others to get ready for the imminent showdown at the box canyon known as the Devil's Gate. Time was passing in a haze of twanging nerves.

The six outlaws had risen early.

They had set off from the hideout on Buffalo Creek the day before and had camped in a draw two hour's ride short of the Circle K ranch.

Leroy Starr had delayed his plans for two days in order to strengthen his gang. With Lopez still languishing in the Casper jailhouse, and Indian Joe decamped to the Happy Hunting Grounds, he needed more men. They could only be hired in Kaycee.

Hawk Wagoner and his buddy Mace Fargo were more than willing to sign up once they learned of the outlaw queen's betrayal. Becoming members of the notorious Starrbreakers was a distinct rise in fortunes for the seedy duo. Saloon brawlers to gun-toting outlaws would bring respect and a thicker billfold.

Starr wanted to reach the edge of Circle K land as dawn was breaking. He wanted to suss out the lie of the unfamiliar terrain. Grey shadows quickly faded as the sun rose above the eastern horizon. The gang leader was counting on their prize haul being corralled separately from the main grazing herds in preparation for breeding.

Scattered groups of grazing longhorns soon hove into view: a surefire clue that they were nearing their quarry.

'Keep your eyes peeled, boys,' he hissed, reining in his mount to a gentle canter. 'And your guns handy. Cain't be far now.'

Eagle eyes scanned the terrain, searching for sign of their bulky quarry.

It was Bob Luman who spotted the entrance to the Devil's Gate. He jabbed a finger towards the narrow gap in the red sandstone cliffs.

'Over there, boss,' he crowed. 'Looks mighty like some hefty beasts grazing in that box canyon.'

The line of riders reined to a halt.

'Could be you're right, Beavertail,' agreed Starr, nodding. 'Let's take a closer look.'

None of them heeded the low yet penetrating ululation wafting across the landscape. Just another owl calling to its mate.

But it was the signal for the hidden riders of the Circle K to ready themselves for the next phase of their plan.

Drew peeped round the side of a boulder. Five minutes later he saw the cluster of riders gingerly approaching the entrance to the short canyon. It was barely more than a hundred yards deep, but sufficient to trap the gang inside.

'It's Starr and his boys,' he whispered to Frank Kendrick, who was lying alongside. 'I'd recognize that arrogant kisser anywhere. And looks like he's brought in reinforcements.'

Kendrick slid down the back of the slanting layer of grey rock to where a wagon and team were waiting. Arkansas Charley was sitting on the bench seat. In the bed lay Ben Sharp and another hand, merely referred to as Blackie on account of his bushy moustache of the same colour.

'Soon as Rooster gives another owl hoot,' he stressed brusquely, 'get this heap across the entrance to the Gate.' The tension was evident from the beads of sweat coating his brow.

'Where's Gabby?' asked the driver. 'Ain't seen her since we left the ranch.'

'She insisted on driving the other wagon across from the far side.' Frank's concerned reply was met by an equally sceptical grimace from Sharp, whose puckered features needed no interpretation. 'You know my sister, Ben. She don't take no for an answer.'

'Anyone with her?' asked Blackie.

'Rooster put his foot down and persuaded her to let him drive.'

'That old-timer sure knows his onions,' chuckled Razor Sharp. The others gave a nervous laugh at the joke as he continued: 'The north side of the entrance affords the best view into the Devil's Gate once the rustlers have passed through the entrance.'

'Rooster'll take good care of her,' consoled Blackie, sensing the boss's trepidation regarding his sister's safety.

Frank responded with a grateful nod. But he was not convinced.

THIRTEEN

THE DEVIL'S GATE

Meanwhile, the gang sat awhile between the rising stoops of rock on either side of the Gate. Swivelling heads scanned the immediate locality. But the cowboys were well concealed.

Silence reigned. Everybody held their breath. This was the moment of truth. Would Starr accept the bait? Each man willed the outlaws to press ahead, lured by the prospect of easy pickings.

'What we waitin' fer?' asked an impatient Bull Montane. It was as if he had an affinity with the creatures after which he was named. 'Them critters are just waitin' for us to haul 'em outa there.'

Starr agreed. Then he turned to address Hawk Wagoner. 'You stay here with the mules and keep an eye open for any unwelcome visitors.' Brimful of confidence, Starr kicked off towards the looming entrance of the Devil's Gate. 'OK boys, let's go get 'em!'

Behind the concealing boulders, Drew cursed. He'd forgotten all about that darned mule train.

'So you were right after all, Belle,' he muttered under his breath.

But Frank Kendrick had heard the muttered aside. He angled a puzzled look towards his new confederate.

'You talkin' about Belle Sherman of the Bee Hive saloon?' he enquired. 'Didn't know you two were acquainted.'

'She was the real brains behind this outfit,' Drew mumbled. 'But Starr gunned her down when she tried to pull out by helping me escape.' He felt uncomfortable talking about the incident. Nor had he any intention of revealing the true nature of his close association with the Outlaw Queen.

He was saved from any further discomfiture when Rooster Langley's signal drifted across from the far side of the Gate.

The gang must be on the move. Backs stiffened, ready for action. A buzzard cawed, Meadowlarks twittered. More time passed before the second call informed them that the gang were well inside the canyon.

This was the moment when they should have driven the wagons across the entrance. But they had to get rid of the guard first.

'Keep me covered while I take him out,' snapped Drew firmly. Frank offered no objection. This was a job for a professional gunman.

The lawman slid down the back of the rock slab

and moved cautiously around behind the point where Wagoner was sitting astride his horse. Drew was counting on the custodian's attention being focused wholly on his buddies. Cat-footing across the open stretch, he approached the outlaw with the easy grace of a mountain lion.

But some sixth sense alerted the rider. He swung round. Witnessing the sudden and unexpected danger to the gang's plans, he grabbed for his pistol. Drew already had his palmed. There was no time for any chivalric display of honour. It was a question of kill or be killed. Drew chose the former.

Two bullets crashed from the raised barrel of the Colt .45 in his left hand. Wagoner threw up his arms and tumbled over the back of his mount.

The ruckus was enough for Frank Kendrick. There was no more time to lose.

'All right, boys!' The rancher's hoarse exclamation was riven by the strain of the moment. 'This it. And make every shot count.'

'Yehaaaaaaah!'

Razor Sharp's strident cry was accompanied by an equally penetrating crack of the bullwhip. The team leapt forward, hauling the wagon out into the open. Slapping leathers urged the horses around the rocky outcrops. Rooster joined him at the same time to block the exit from the Devil's Gate.

Inside the compact box canyon, Starr's plan appeared to be working perfectly. But the two pistol shots instantly damped his euphoria.

'It's a trap,' shouted Mace Fargo. Hauling out his

six-shooter, the outlaw leaped from the saddle and ducked down behind a corral post.

His partner was not so fortunate. Rather slow and lumbering, Montane had failed to heed the urgent warning. A well-placed shot from Rooster Langley's rifle lifted him out of the saddle. It was a killing shot.

'Take cover, boys,' Starr exhorted, pumping off a full chamber towards the entrance where the wagons now blocked his escape.

A mirthless smile creased his twisted visage as a pained cry told him that one of the slugs had struck home. At the same time, his mind was struggling to figure out how the cowboys had known they were coming. Apart from the gang, no one else had been in on the job.

Bullets flew past his head, chewing large slivers of wood from the corral posts. The dilemma was now merely speculative compared to their current problem. He thrust it aside to concentrate on returning fire.

Although they were not gunslingers by profession, the cowboys were adept shots. Their weapons soon became hot from constant use.

But not everything had gone their way. First to go down was Arkansas Charley, who had received a bullet in the shoulder. Although not judged to be a serious injury, it removed him from the battleground.

'Watch you don't hit the bulls,' yelled Frank above the din of gunfire. Preventing the theft was the main reason he had agreed to back Drew Henry's effort to break up the gang. 'Those fellas are worth a president's ransom.'

Fifteen minutes passed with neither side gaining the initiative. But the attackers had the upper hand. They could keep the Starrbreakers holed up indefinitely until reinforcements in the form of the law could be summoned.

Leroy cast a searching look around the small canyon. Like a snaking rope, a silver cataract plunged over its back rim. Disappearing into a pool at the base of the cliff, it offered a water supply, but no feasible exit. The only way out of the Devil's Gate was through the front door.

Leroy knew that he had to do something if he was to survive. The notion of surrendering merely to attend his own necktie party was given short shrift. It was escape to fight another day, or go down in a blaze of glory. A sharp cry from the gaping mouth of Rusty Laverne told him that yet another of his men had bitten the dust.

But the rancher's bellowed warning to his men had given the gang boss an idea. He could use the huge weight of the burly animals to his advantage.

It was the only way out.

Again the riddle concerning the source of betrayal dogged Starr's thoughts. It sure was a poser. None of the gang would have blabbed. They knew what the outcome would be – a bullet in the head!

So how had they been found out? Surely that skulking lawdog couldn't have survived the fall into the ravine? And what about Belle? Had she somehow managed to get over the rockfall and reach help, with a gunshot injury? It seemed highly unlikely.

That question would have to be shelved for the time being. But once he had escaped and set up a new gang, the matter would certainly be addressed. He shook off the torpor of melancholy that threatened to overwhelm his whole being, and focused on getting out of this mess with his skin intact.

Squinting through the dusty murk, his uneasy gaze descried that only himself and Beavertail Bob Luman were left standing. The ex-convict was reloading his rifle on the far side of the corral. Starr hurried around the back of the z-shaped line of fencing.

'The only way outa here is to stampede the bulls and follow them out,' the gang boss stuttered. His breath rasped harshly in a throat made sore from too much dust as well as the acute tension.

Luman nodded his understanding. Any regrets he might have harboured regarding his joining up with the Starrbreakers were now superfluous. All that mattered was survival to fight another day.

'Open the gate while I get them moving,' added Starr. 'Shouldn't be difficult. The critters are already more skittish than a Mexican jumping bean.' As if in agreement, the animals bawled, angrily stamping their hoofs. 'A couple more shots up their asses should set 'em off.'

Keeping his back bent low, Luman scuttled round to the front of the corral and hauled out the retaining poles. Two shots rang out from the back of the enclosure. It was enough to precipitate a full-blown charge. All three bulls lumbered into motion at the same time. Once freed from the the confines of the corral, they surged towards the entrance.

Heads down, the crazed beasts were mindless of any obstruction in their way. The ground rumbled and shook as three tons of prime breeding stock lurched forward. Clouds of yellow dust obscured the full horror of the rapidly approaching onslaught. Only in the last few seconds did the dire nature of their predicamant strike the defending cowmen.

By then it was too late.

FOURTEEN

FINAL ACCOUNT

The flimsy barricades were no hindrance to rampaging bulls. With barely a pause they smashed into the wagons. That on the right of the entrance received the most direct hit.

First to witness the sudden attack was Blackie.

'Look out!' he yelled above the roaring pandemonium. 'They've stampeded the bulls.' Pure instinct caused the stocky cowpoke to dive head first off the wagon. He landed in a heap, winded but otherwise unhurt.

His partner was not so lucky. Razor Sharp was thrown the wrong way. He didn't stand a chance. Thrashing hoofs hammered him into the ground. Blackie somehow managed to get off a few shots that struck one of the rampaging beasts. The creature let out a manic bellow, tumbling head over heels before shuddering to a halt amidst the wreckage of the wagon.

By sheer luck, the other wagon only suffered a glancing blow. The two occupants were forced to discard their weapons as they clung desperately to the sides.

'Get clear, Gabby!' hollered the veteran cook, rummaging around for his trusty Springfield. The girl hesitated, disorientated by the tumult surrounding her. To Rooster Langley, however, it was like being back in action. A grim smile tugged at the seamed face. 'Don't just stand there, gal. Jump!' The urgent reiteration jerked Gabby's blinkered mind back to the reality of their dire situation.

She leapt clear just as Langley found his rifle. As he raised the long gun to his shoulder his aim was obscured by the thicks clouds of dust. A blurred image suddenly appeared in front of him. He pulled the trigger. A hat lifted from the rider's head.

Following closely behind the charging bulls, the two surviving outlaws fired their revolvers at anything that moved. Starr ducked low as his hat disappeared. It was yet another close hair-parting. But he kept going. Orange tongues of flame spat from the outlaw's six-gun as the looming apparition hove out of the murky gloom.

Rooster clutched at his chest. A second bullet almost tore his head off. The rider shot past. Ever the one to grab an opportunity when presented, the outlaw's grit-scoured eyes lit upon the confused girl. Here was a chance to get out of this fracas unscathed. And with a hostage as insurance.

Reaching out, he slowed his mount to scoop up

the tottering female, tossing her across the saddle horn. Brought to her senses by the imminent danger, Gabby struggled to free herself.

A feral growl bubbled in Starr's throat. With his free hand, he brought the butt of his revolver down across the girl's head.

'That'll keep you quiet for a spell, missy,' he spat out, 'until I can get clear of this viper's nest.'

Seeing his sister being abducted, Frank Kendrick emitted a pained roar.

'Noooooo!' he yelled.

He brought his gun up.

'Don't shoot, Frank, you might hit Gabby.' Drew Henry's right hand knocked the rifle aside. 'See to the wounded men. I'll bring her back.' Frank eyed him askance. 'It's my job, remember?' stressed the lawman. He reached into his vest pocket, extracted a shiny metal star and pinned it on in full view. A proud finger poked at the glittering badge of office. 'Special Investigator – one of the true Bad Boys!'

A diamond hardness matched with icy determination imbued his whole being as Drew moved across to his horse.

Mounting up, he turned a more composed face towards the drawn features of the Circle K rancher. 'Don't worry, Frank,' he murmured softly. 'I'll bring her back safe and sound. Or die trying.'

Then with a raised hand of farewell, he spurred off in pursuit of Leroy Starr and his captive.

During the breakout from the Devil's Gate, Bob

Luman had kept a short distance behind the gang leader. Once they had ridden beyond the scene of carnage, he drew level.

'That gal's gonna slow us down,' he said, voicing his doubts as to the efficacy of Starr's choice of an insurance policy. 'Sure you don't wanna ditch her? One of them critters is followin' us.'

A caustic glower shot across the intervening space separating the duo. Starr didn't cotton to challenges being expressed about his decisions, although he was willing to concede that an unwilling passenger was a distinct hindrance to progress.

'None of them turkeys will dare come too close with the girl's life being at stake. Soon as we reach the hideout on Buffalo Creek, we'll dump her.' A lurid grin split the coarse features. 'In the nearest ravine . . . after we've had some fun, naturally.'

Luman liked that. But it was his next observation that wiped the smirking expression from Starr's leery visage.

'You might feel different knowin' it's that skunk who was impersonatin' me.'

So that was it. The blasted Judas had somehow managed to escape from Antelope Canyon. Now he knew how those critters had learned about their prize stock being rustled.

'Maybe I should deter this lunkhead from tryin' to be a hero,' suggested Luman, fingering one of his Smith & Wesson Schofields.

Starr responded with a curt nod. 'Make sure it's permanent.'

'Don't worry, boss, I got a score to settle with that varmint. The only place he's goin' is to Hell on a one-way ticket.' He swung his horse around. 'See yuh later.'

Drew could see the two riders ahead. He didn't want to get too close because of Gabby. Five minutes later he noticed that there was only one rider. Narrowed eyes registered his puzzlement. Then he had it figured.

They must have spotted him. And one of the rats was lying in wait ready to ambush him. Drew's face set like stone. Well, two can play at that game.

Eyes peeled, he slowed the cow pony to a gentle trot. Up ahead were a cluster of rocks. The ideal place of concealment for a bushwhacker. Drew pulled off the trail and circled around behind the rocks. Keeping to the cover of the surrounding bushes, he tethered his mount and climbed up above where he figured the sniper would be concealed.

And there he was. The real Bob Luman, rifle at the ready.

Gingerly Drew crept down until he was just behind the ex-convict.

'Drop your gun and turn around!'

Luman's whole body tensed up. He'd been suckered. And it rankled. Prudence and thought for the consquences evaporated. Yet again this guy had made a fool of him. Well, it was the last time. Beavertail Bob swung in a single fluid motion, bringing his rifle to bare.

It was a futile manoeuvre. And doomed to failure.

Three bullets struck him in the chest.

Drew didn't pause to check his victim. Bob Luman was not about to get up.

Two miles ahead, Leroy Starr smiled to himself, visibly relaxing. The tension flowed out of his tight muscles. From here on it would all be plain sailing. Once back at the ranch he would salvage anything worthwhile and head south for New Mexico with Luman and make a fresh start.

But as the sun sank lower in the sky, Starr began to fear the worst. Where was Luman? Why had he not caught up? There was only one possible answer.

The crafty lawman must have somehow gotten the better of the ex-convict. And was even now dogging his trail.

But Leroy Starr had not risen to become the feared leader of the infamous Wyoming Starrbreakers by sitting back and allowing himself to be outfoxed. An angle was needed to throw the lawman on to a false scent.

Scanning the immediate surroundings, his keen gaze searched for what he had in mind. The rolling terrain undulated like an ocean's swell. Clusters of rocky outcrops lined the little-used trail rising out of the grassy landscape. A herd of grazing antelope suddenly veered away from the approaching rider. The side draw down which they disappeared gave Starr the opening he needed.

He swung the horse along the narrow rift, making sure that his trail was well marked. The girl shuffled in front. After she had regained consciousness, he had gagged and tethered her securely to the saddle while he sat behind atop the bedroll.

'Keep still, girl,' he snapped waspishly, tugging down on her long hair. 'Else I'll do fer yuh here and now.' The wriggling subsided. But she maintained a stiffly arrogant back to assert her disdain for her kidnapper.

The draw meandered between low crags. After ten minutes, the outlaw reined up and dismounted. Dragging the girl off, he tossed her aside like an old shirt. Then he slapped the horse on the rump. The animal jumped forward, continuing along the draw and out of sight round the next bend. Starr brushed out his and the girl's boot tracks, then hid behind a cluster of rocks.

And waited.

It was another half-hour before the steady plod of approaching hoofs warned him that the pursuer was getting close. A warped grin split his darkly malign features. The skunk had nibbled at the bait. He checked the girl's bonds and palmed his revolver.

Drew sauntered past, his eyes fastened on to the clearly defined trail of the horse. Once passed, Starr emerged from cover.

'Hold it right there, mister.'

The triumph was evident in his arrogant tone. This time it was Drew who had been tricked. A lurid curse burst from the Bad Boy's throat. He should had given the gang leader more credit. Too late now.

'Now unbuckle that fancy rig and toss it aside.' Starr

cranked back the hammer to full cock. 'And don't try anything funny if'n you don't want the girl chewin' on a lead sandwich. Now step down, slow and easy.'

Drew was forced to obey.

But Starr had omitted to bind up his captive's legs. Gabby quietly stumbled to her feet and crept out from behind the rocks. Starr had his back to her. His entire wrathful attention was focused on the object of his derision.

Hardly daring to breathe, Gabby stole up behind the hovering outlaw.

But the sun was in the wrong place. Her shadow gave the ploy away. A manic growl rumbled in Starr's throat as he swung round, slamming a scything haymaker at the girl's head. The tight gag across her mouth cut off the scream of pain. Blood poured from a split lip as she went down.

However, the brave act gave Drew the chance he needed. Diving to one side, he fumbled at the thong securing one of his revolvers. Starr's gun hand swung to face the unexpected challenge.

Both shooters erupted together. Flame and death poured forth simultaneously. A second shot followed almost immediately. Smoke enveloping the protagonists drifted in the static air.

But it was Starr who sank to his knees. A look of stupefaction clouded his bloodless features as he peered at the red stain spreading across his shirt front. Then slowly, he keeled over and lay still.

Drew scrambled to his feet and rushed over to his stricken saviour.

'You all right, honey?' he murmured taking her in his arms. 'I'd have been buzzard bait if'n you hadn't got involved.'

Gabby tore off the constricting gag. Lifting a finger, she stilled the flow of words, then leaned up and kissed him full on the mouth.

After coming up for air, Drew Henry steadied his roaring heartbeat. A single teardrop etched a path through the dark stubble of his right cheek. He quickly brushed it aside. A memory evoked, but not forgotten.

Then he stammered out in a rather hoarse voice, 'Is that job still on offer?'

The girl's reply was an enchanting smile.

'That and much more . . . if'n you've a mind?'